Rex Stout's Nero Wolfe and Archie Goodwin Triumphantly Return in Robert Goldsborough's *Murder in E Minor*

"Archie's narration is as breezy and witty as we all remember it to be . . . Nero Wolfe has never been in better form than he is in this case."
—*Alfred Hitchcock's Mystery Magazine*

"Nero Wolfe lives again! *Murder in E Minor* is remarkably faithful in tone and detail to Stout's originals."
—*Philadelphia Daily News*

"Nero Wolfe lives. . . . Goldsborough has picked up the baton and he misses nary a beat."
—New York *Daily News*

"Goldsborough has picked up where Stout left off . . . With the familiar order, 'Archie, your notebook. Instructions,' the chase is under way." —*Pittsburgh Press*

"Goldsborough has been exceedingly careful in the restoration of Nero and Archie . . . *Murder in E Minor* tells an entertaining story, but it is Nero and Archie who elevate it to special status."
—*Chicago Sun-Times*

"The principal pleasure of *Murder in E Minor* is in its frank appeal to our nostalgia. Weighing in at 'a seventh of a ton' and with an ego to match, Wolfe remains the ultimate eccentric . . . Are they back for good? The answer Wolfe gives here will please all once and future fans: 'I've always viewed investigative work as an integral part of my existence. And at the present time I have no plans to terminate my existence.'" —*Newsweek*

Please turn the page for an excerpt from *MURDER IN E MINOR* . . .

Murder in E Minor

The doorway led into a good-sized library with a
fireplace, a grand piano, and an Oriental rug. The
body was lying facedown near a high, monk-style
writing desk. Milan Stevens was dead, and it wasn't
hard to figure out why: the back of his white shirt
was stained dark red, and a fancy, long-handled
letter opener lay a few feet away. A softcover book lay
open on the monk's desk, and I covered my hand
with my handkerchief as I turned the pages. It
was music, plus a lot of penciled notations that might
as well have been in Urdu. For the record, the cover
sheet said "Symphony No. 4 in E Minor, for
Orchestra, by Johannes Brahms, Op. 98." I went back
to the study and dialed the number I know best.
Wolfe answered after one ring.
"Stevens is dead. Stabbed in his study.
I'm there now, with Maria, and I'm about to call the
police. Instructions?"
I could hear him draw in air and let it out slowly.
"No," he said. "I suppose you'll have to go to
headquarters?"
"Without question," I said.
"I'll report first thing in the morning, if they let me
out by then."
"Very well," Wolfe said with disgust. "Have you
eaten?"

AND SO BEGINS A NEW MYSTERY FOR REX
STOUT'S NERO WOLFE AND ARCHIE
GOODWIN, WRITTEN WITH ACCLAIMED
AUTHENTICITY BY NERO WOLFE EXPERT
ROBERT GOLDSBOROUGH

· *A NERO WOLFE MYSTERY* ·

MURDER
IN E MINOR

Robert Goldsborough

BANTAM BOOKS

TORONTO · NEW YORK · LONDON · SYDNEY · AUCKLAND

The author wishes to thank the estate of
the late Rex Stout for its cooperation and
encouragement

MURDER IN E MINOR
A Bantam Book
Bantam hardcover edition / April 1986
A main selection of the Mystery Book Club August 1986
Bantam paperback edition / March 1987
3 printings through September 1988

Library of Congress Cataloging-in-Publication Data
Goldsborough, Robert.
    Murder in E minor.

    I. Title.
PS3557.03849M8   1986   813.54   85-48045
ISBN 0-553-27938-6

Published simultaneously in the United States and Canada

Bantam Books are published by Bantam Books, a division of Bantam
Doubleday Dell Publishing Group, Inc. Its trademark, consisting of the
words "Bantam Books" and the portrayal of a rooster, is Registered in
U.S. Patent and Trademark Office and in other countries. Marca
Registrada. Bantam Books, 666 Fifth Avenue, New York, New York 10103.

PRINTED IN THE UNITED STATES OF AMERICA

O   12 11 10 9 8 7 6 5 4 3

In memory of my mother,
who first introduced me to Nero Wolfe
and Archie Goodwin.

FOREWORD

I realize that a lot was written and broadcast about the case that follows, not just in New York, but across the country. However, nobody, not even Lon Cohen's *Gazette*, had the space or the knowledge to come anywhere close to giving the whole account. I didn't think it would ever get printed anywhere, for that matter. Let me explain. Because this episode was such a personal one for Nero Wolfe, he didn't feel I ought to write about it. And because he signs my weekly checks, I went along with him, at least for a while. Even Wolfe can be worn down by badgering, though. It took me a long time (I didn't bring the subject up all that often), but he finally gave in, years after the fact. He didn't give me any reasons, he just nodded, probably to shut me up. Now you know.

ARCHIE GOODWIN

1

Nero Wolfe and I have argued for years about whether the client who makes his first visit to us before or after noon is more likely to provide an interesting—and lucrative—case. Wolfe contends that the average person is incapable of making a rational decision, such as hiring him, until he or she has had a minimum of two substantial meals that day. My own feeling is that the caller with the greater potential is the one who has spent the night agonizing, finally realizes at dawn that Wolfe is the answer, and does something about it fast. I'll leave it to you to decide, based on our past experience, which of us has it better pegged.

I'd have been more smug about the timing of Maria Radovich's call that rainy morning if I'd thought there was even one chance in twenty that Wolfe would see her, let alone go back to work. It had been more than two years since Orrie Cather committed suicide—with Wolfe's blessing and mine. At the time, the realization that one of his longtime standbys had murdered three

2 · ROBERT GOLDSBOROUGH

people didn't seem to bother Wolfe, but since then I had come to see that the whole business had rocked him pretty good. He would never admit it, of course, with that ego fit for his seventh of a ton, but he was still stung that someone who for years had sat at his table, drunk his liquor, and followed his orders could be a cool and deliberate killer. And even though the D.A. had reinstated both our licenses shortly after Orrie's death, Wolfe had stuck his head in the sand and still hadn't pulled it out. I tried needling him back to work, a tactic that had been successful in the past, but I got stonewalled, to use a word he hates.

"Archie," he would say, looking up from his book, "as I have told you many times, one of your most commendable attributes through the years has been your ability to badger me into working. That former asset is now a liability. You may goad me if you wish, but it is futile. I will not take the bait. And desist using the word 'retired.' I prefer to say that I have withdrawn from practice." And with that, he would return to his book, which currently was a rereading of *Emma* by Jane Austen.

It wasn't that we did not have opportunities. One well-fixed Larchmont widow offered twenty grand for starters if Wolfe would find out who poisoned her chauffeur, and I couldn't even get him to see her. The murder was never solved, although I leaned toward the live-in maid, who was losing out in a triangle to the gardener's daughter. Then there was the Wall Street money man—you'd know his name right off—who said Wolfe could set his own price if only we'd investigate his son's death. The police and the coroner had called it a suicide, but the father was convinced it was a narcotics-related murder. Wolfe politely but firmly turned the man down in a ten-minute conversation in the office, and the kid's death went on the books as a suicide.

I couldn't even use the money angle to stir him. On

a few of our last big cases, Wolfe insisted on having the payments spread over a long period, so that a series of checks—some of them biggies—rolled in every month. That, coupled with a bunch of good investments, gave him a cash flow that was easily sufficient to operate the old brownstone on West Thirty-fifth Street near the Hudson that has been home to me for more than half my life. And operating the brownstone doesn't come cheap, because Nero Wolfe has costly tastes. They include my salary as his confidential assistant, errand boy, and—until two years ago—man of action, as well as those of Theodore Horstmann, nurse to the ten thousand orchids Wolfe grows in the plant rooms up on the roof, and Fritz Brenner, on whom I would bet in a cook-off against any other chef in the universe.

I still had the standard chores, such as maintaining the orchid germination records, paying the bills, figuring the taxes, and handling Wolfe's correspondence. But I had lots of free time now, and Wolfe didn't object to a little free-lancing. I did occasional work for Del Bascomb, a first-rate local operative, and also teamed with Saul Panzer on a couple of jobs, including the Masters kidnapping case, which you may have read about. Wolfe went so far as to compliment me on that one, so at least I knew he still read about crime, although he refused to let me talk about it in his presence anymore.

Other than having put his brain in the deep freeze, Wolfe kept his routine pretty much the same as ever: breakfast on a tray in his room; four hours a day—9 to 11 A.M. and 4 to 6 P.M.—in the plant rooms with Theodore; long conferences with Fritz on menus and food preparation; and the best meals in Manhattan. The rest of the time, he was in his oversized chair behind his desk in the office reading and drinking beer. And refusing to work.

Maria Radovich's call came at nine-ten on Tuesday morning, which meant Wolfe was up with the plants. Fritz was in the kitchen working on one of Wolfe's favorite lunches, sweetbreads in bechamel sauce and truffles. I answered at my desk, where I was balancing the checkbook.

"Nero Wolfe's residence. Archie Goodwin speaking."

"I need to see Mr. Wolfe—today. May I make an appointment?" It was the voice of a young woman, shaky, and with an accent that seemed familiar to me.

"I'm sorry, but Mr. Wolfe isn't consulting at the present time," I said, repeating a line I had grown to hate.

"Please, it's important that I see him. I think my—"

"Look, Mr. Wolfe isn't seeing anyone, honest. I can suggest some agencies if you're looking for a private investigator."

"No, I want Mr. Nero Wolfe. My uncle has spoken of him, and I am sure he would want to help. My uncle knew Mr. Wolfe many years ago in Montenegro, and—"

"Where?" I barked it out.

"In Montenegro. They grew up there together. And now I am frightened about my uncle . . ."

Ever since it became widely known that Wolfe had retired—make that "withdrawn from practice"—would-be clients had cooked up some dandy stories to try to get him working again. I was on their side, but I knew Wolfe well enough to realize that almost nothing would bring him back to life. This was the first time, though, that anyone had been ingenious enough to come up with a Montenegro angle, and I admire ingenuity.

"I'm sorry to hear that you're scared," I said, "but Mr. Wolfe is pretty hard-hearted. I've got a reputation as a softie, though. How soon can your uncle be here? I'm Mr. Wolfe's confidential assistant, and I'll be glad to see him, Miss . . ."

"Radovich, Maria Radovich. Yes, I recognized your

name. My uncle doesn't know I am calling. He would be angry. But I will come right away, if it's all right."

I assured her it was indeed all right and hung up, staring at the open checkbook. It was a long shot, no question, but if I had anything to lose by talking to her, I couldn't see it. And just maybe, the Montenegro bit was for real. Montenegro, in case you don't know, is a small piece of Yugoslavia, and it's where Wolfe comes from. He still has relatives there; I send checks to three of them every month. But as for old friends, I doubted any were still alive. His closest friend ever, Marko Vukcic, had been murdered years ago, and the upshot was that Wolfe and I went tramping off to the Montenegrin mountains to avenge his death. And although Wolfe was anything but gabby about his past, I figured I knew just about enough to eliminate the possibility of a close comrade popping up. But there's no law against hoping.

I got a good, leisurely look at her through the one-way glass in the front door as she stood in the drizzle ringing our bell. Dark-haired, dark-eyed, and slender, she had a touch of Mia Farrow in her face. And like Farrow in several of her roles, she seemed frightened and unsure. But looking through the glass, I was convinced that with Maria Radovich, it was no act.

She jumped when I opened the door. "Oh! Mr. Goodwin?"

"The selfsame," I answered with a slight bow and an earnest smile. "And you are Maria Radovich, I presume? Please come in out of the twenty-percent chance of showers."

I hung her trench coat on the hall rack and motioned toward the office. Walking behind her, I could see that her figure, set off by a skirt of fashionable length, was a bit fuller than I remembered Mia Farrow's to be, and that was okay with me.

"Mr. Wolfe doesn't come down to the office for another hour and ten minutes," I said, motioning to the yellow chair nearest my desk. "Which is fine, because he wouldn't see you anyway. At least not right now. He thinks he's retired from the detective business. But I'm not." I flipped open my notebook and swiveled to face her.

"I'm sure if Mr. Wolfe knew about my uncle's trouble, he would want to do something right away," she said, twisting a scarf in her lap and leaning forward tensely.

"You don't know him, Miss Radovich. He can be immovable, irascible, and exasperating when he wants to, which is most of the time. I'm afraid you're stuck with me, at least for now. Maybe we can get Mr. Wolfe interested later, but to do that, I've got to know everything. Like for starters, who is your uncle and why are you worried about him?"

"He is my great-uncle, really," she answered, still using only the front quarter of the chair cushion. "And he is very well-known. Milan Stevens. I am sure you have heard of him—he is music director, some people say conductor, of the New York Symphony."

Not wanting to look stupid or disappoint her, or both, I nodded. I've been to the Symphony four or five times, always with Lily Rowan, and it was always her idea. Milan Stevens may have been the conductor one or more of those times, but I wouldn't take an oath on it. The name was only vaguely familiar.

"Mr. Goodwin, for the last two weeks my uncle has been getting letters in the mail—awful, vile letters. I think someone may want to kill him, but he just throws the letters away. I am frightened. I am sure that—"

"How many letters have there been, Miss Radovich? Do you have any of them?"

She nodded and reached into the shoulder bag she had set on the floor. "Three so far, all the same." She handed the crumpled sheets over, along with their envelopes, and I spread them on my desk. Each was on six-by-nine-inch notepaper, plain white, the kind from an inexpensive tear-off pad. They were hand-printed, in all caps, with a black felt-tip pen. One read:

MAESTRO
QUIT THE PODIUM NOW! YOU ARE
DOING DAMAGE TO A GREAT ORCHESTRA
PUT DOWN THE BATON AND GET OUT
IF YOU DON'T LEAVE ON YOUR OWN,
YOU WILL BE REMOVED—PERMANENTLY!

In fact, all three weren't exactly alike. The wording differed, though only slightly. The "on your own" in the last sentence was missing from one note, and the first sentence didn't have an exclamation point in another. Maria had lightly penciled the numbers one, two, and three on the back of each to indicate the order in which they were received. The envelopes were of a similar ordinary stock, each hand-printed to Milan Stevens at an address in the East Seventies. "His apartment?" I asked.

Maria nodded. "Yes, he and I have lived there since we came to this country, a little over two years ago."

"Miss Radovich, before we talk more about these notes, tell me about your uncle, and yourself. First, you said on the phone that he and Mr. Wolfe knew each other in Montenegro."

She eased back into the chair and nodded. "Yes, my uncle—his real name is Stefanovic, Milos Stefanovic. We are from Yugoslavia. I was born in Belgrade, but my uncle is a Montenegrin. That's a place on the Adriatic. But of course I don't have to tell you that—I'm sure you know all about it from Mr. Wolfe.

"My uncle's been a musician and conductor all over Europe—Italy, Austria, Germany. He was conducting in London last, before we came here. But long ago, he did some fighting in Montenegro. I know little of it, but I think he was involved in an independence movement. He doesn't like to talk about that at all, and he never mentioned Mr. Wolfe to me until one time when his picture was in the papers. It was something to do with a murder or a suicide—I think maybe your picture was there too?"

I nodded. That would have been when Orrie died. "What did your uncle say about Mr. Wolfe?"

"I gather they had lost touch over the years. But he didn't seem at all interested in trying to reach Mr. Wolfe. At the time I said, 'How wonderful that such an old friend is right here. What a surprise! You'll call him, of course?' But Uncle Milos said no, that was part of the past. And I got the idea from the way he acted that they must have had some kind of difference. But that was so long ago!"

"If you sensed your uncle was unfriendly toward Mr. Wolfe, what made you call?"

"After he told me about knowing Mr. Wolfe back in Montenegro, Uncle Milos kept looking at the picture in the paper and nodding his head. He said to me, 'He had the finest mind I have ever known. I wish I could say the same for his disposition.' "

I held back a smile. "But you got the impression that your uncle and Mr. Wolfe were close at one time?"

"Absolutely," Maria said. "Uncle Milos told me they had been through some great difficulty together. He even showed me this picture from an old scrapbook." She reached again into her bag and handed me a gray-toned photograph mounted on cardboard and ragged around the edges.

They certainly fit my conception of a band of guerrillas, although none looked to be out of his teens. There were nine in all, posed in front of a high stone wall, four kneeling in front and five standing behind them.

Some were wearing long overcoats, others had on woolen shirts, and two wore what I think of as World War I helmets. I spotted Wolfe instantly, of course. He was second from the left in the back row, with his hands behind his back and a bandolier slung over one shoulder. His hair was darker then, and he weighed at least one hundred pounds less, but the face was remarkably similar to the one I had looked at across the dinner table last night. And his glare had the same intensity, coming at me from a faded picture, that it does in the office when he thinks I'm badgering him.

To Wolfe's right in the photo was Marko Vukcic, holding a rifle loosely at his side. "Which one's your uncle?" I asked Maria.

She leaned close enough so I could smell her perfume and pointed to one of the kneelers in front. He was dark-haired and intense like most of the others, but he appeared smaller than most of them. None of the nine, though, looked as if he were trying to win a congeniality contest. If they were as tough as they appeared, I'm glad I wasn't fighting against them.

"This picture was taken up in the mountains," Maria said. "Uncle Milos only showed it to me to point out Mr. Wolfe, but he wouldn't talk any more about the other men or what they were doing."

"Not going to a picnic," I said. "I'd like to hang onto this for a while. Now, what about you, Miss Radovich? How does it happen you're living with a great-uncle?"

She told me about how her mother, a widow, had died when she was a child in Yugoslavia, and that Stefanovic, her mother's uncle, had legally adopted her. Divorced and without children, he was happy to have the companionship of a nine-year-old. Maria said he gave her all the love of a parent, albeit a strict one, taking her with him as he moved around Europe to increasingly better and more prestigious conducting jobs. At some time before moving to England, he had changed his name to Stevens—she couldn't remember exactly when. It was while they were living in London that he was picked as the new conductor, or music director if you prefer, of the New York Symphony. Maria, who by that time was twenty-three, made the move with him, and she was now a dancer with a small troupe in New York.

"Mr. Goodwin," she said, leaning forward and tensing again, "my uncle has worked hard all his life to get the kind of position and recognition he has today. Now somebody is trying to take it away from him." Her hand gripped my forearm.

"Why not just go to the police?" I asked with a shrug.

"I suggested that to Uncle Milos, and he became very angry. He said it would leak out to the newspapers and cause a scandal at the Symphony, that the publicity would be harmful to him and the orchestra. He says these notes are from a crazy person, or maybe someone playing a prank. I was with him when he opened the first one, or I might not know about any of this. He read it and said something that means 'stupid' in Serbo-Croatian, then crumpled the note and threw it in the wastebasket. But he hardly spoke the rest of the evening.

"I waited until he left the room to get the note from the basket. It was then that I said we should call the police. He became upset and said it was probably a prankster, or maybe a season-ticket holder who didn't like the music the orchestra had been playing."

"How long until the next note?" I asked.

"I started watching the mail after that. Six days later, we got another envelope printed just like the first one. I didn't open it—I never open my uncle's mail. But again I found the crumpled note in the wastebasket next to his desk in the library. This time I didn't mention it to him, and he said nothing about it to me, but again he seemed distressed.

"The third note came yesterday, six days after the second, and again I found it in the wastebasket. Uncle Milos doesn't know that I've seen the last two notes, or that I've saved all three."

"Miss Radovich, does your uncle have any enemies you know of, anyone who would gain by his leaving the Symphony?"

"The music director of a large orchestra always has his detractors." She took a deep breath. "There are always people who think it can be done better. Some are jealous, others just take pleasure in scoffing at talented people. My uncle does not discuss his work very much at home, but I do know, from him and from others, that he has opposition even within the orchestra. But notes like this, I can't believe—"

"*Someone* is writing them, Miss Radovich. I'd like to hear more about your uncle's opposition, but Mr. Wolfe will be down in just a few minutes, and it's best if you're not here when he comes in. He may get interested in your problem, but you'll have to let me be the one to try getting him interested."

For the third time, Maria dove into her bag. She fished out a wad of bills and thrust it at me. "There's five hundred dollars here," she said. "That is just for agreeing to try to find out who's writing the notes. I can pay another forty-five hundred dollars if you discover the person and get him to stop." Five grand was a long way below what Wolfe usually got as a fee, but I figured that for Maria Radovich, it was probably big bucks. I started to return the money, then I drew back and smiled.

"Fair enough," I said. "If I can get Nero Wolfe to move, we keep this. Otherwise, it goes back to you. Now we've got to get you out of here. You'll be hearing from me soon—one way or the other." I wrote her a receipt for the money, keeping a carbon, and hustled her out to the hall and on with her coat.

My watch said ten fifty-eight as she went down the steps to the street. I rushed back to the office, put the money and receipt in the safe, and arranged Wolfe's morning mail in a pile on his blotter. Included in the stack was one item the carrier hadn't delivered: a faded fifty-year-old photograph.

2

I just had time to get my paper in the typewriter and start on yesterday's dictation when I heard the elevator coming down from the plant rooms. "Good morning, Archie, did you sleep well?" he asked as he walked across to his desk, arranged a raceme of purple Cattleyas in the vase, then settled his bulk into the only chair he likes and rang for beer.

"Yes, sir," I answered, looking up. Despite his size, and we're talking about a seventh of a ton here, I've never gotten used to how efficient Wolfe is when he moves. Somehow, you keep thinking he's going to trip or do something clumsy when he goes around behind his desk, but he never does. Everything is smooth, even graceful—if you can use that word with someone so large. Then there are his clothes. Fat people get a rap for being sloppy, but not Nero Wolfe. Today, as usual, he was wearing a three-piece suit, this one a tan tweed, with a fresh yellow shirt and a brown silk tie with narrow yellow stripes. His wavy hair, still brown but with a healthy dose of gray mixed in, was carefully brushed. He'd never admit it to me or anybody else, but Nero Wolfe spent his share of time in front of the mirror every morning, and that included shaving with a straight razor, something I quit trying years ago when I got tired of the sight of my own blood.

I kept sneaking glances at Wolfe while he riffled through the stack of mail. The photograph was about halfway down, but he took his time getting there, stopping as I knew he would to peruse a seed catalog. I typed on.

"Archie!" It was a high-grade bellow, the first one he'd uncorked in months.

I looked up, feigning surprise.

"Where did this come from?" he asked, jabbing at the picture.

"What's that, sir?" I raised one eyebrow, which always gets him because he can't do it.

"You know very well. How did this get here? What envelope was it in?"

"Oh, *that*. Well, let me think . . . yes, of course, I almost forgot. It was brought by a young woman, nice-looking, too. She thought you might be interested in helping her with a problem."

Wolfe glowered, then leaned forward and studied the photograph. "They must all be dead by now. . . . Two were killed by firing squads, one died in a foolhardy duel, another drowned in the Adriatic. And Marko . . ."

"They're not *all* dead," I put in. "You aren't, not legally anyway, although you've been putting on a good imitation for a couple of years. And there's at least one other living man in that picture."

Wolfe went back to the photograph, this time for more than a minute. "*Stefanovic*." He pronounced it far differently than I would have. "I have no knowledge of his death."

"You win a case of salt-water taffy," I said. "Not only

is he still breathing, but he lives right here in New York. And what's more, he's famous. Of course he's changed his name since you knew him."

Wolfe shot me another glower. His index finger was tracing circles on the arm of the chair, the only outward indication that he was furious. I knew more than he did about something and was forcing him to ask questions, which made it even worse.

"Archie, I have suffered your contumacy for longer than I care to think about." He pursed his lips. "Confound it, report!"

"Yes, sir," I said, maintaining a somber expression. Then I unloaded everything verbatim, from Maria's phone call to the money. When I got to the part about the three notes, I opened the safe and pulled them out, but he refused to give them a glance. During my whole report, he sat with his eyes closed, fingers interlaced on his center mound. He interrupted twice to ask questions. When I was through, he sat in silence, eyes still closed.

After about five minutes, I said, "Are you asleep, or just waiting for me to call in a portrait painter so he can capture your favorite pose?"

"Archie, shut up!" That made it two bellows in one day. I was trying to think up something smart to say that would bring on a third and set a record, but Fritz came in and announced lunch.

Wolfe has a rule, never broken, that business is not to be discussed during meals, and it had been an easy rule to keep for the last two years, since there wasn't any business. That day, though, my mind was on other things and I barely tasted Fritz's superb sweetbreads. Wolfe, however, consumed three helpings at his normal, unhurried pace, while holding forth on the reasons why third parties have been unsuccessful in American elections.

We finally went back to the office for coffee. During

lunch, I decided I'd pushed Wolfe enough and would leave the next move to him. We sat in silence for several minutes, and I was beginning to revise my strategy when he got up and went to the bookshelf. He pulled down the big atlas, lugged it back to his desk, and opened it. He looked at a page, then turned back to the photograph, fingering it gently.

"Archie?" He drew in a bushel of air, then let it out slowly.

"Yes, sir?"

"You know Montenegro, at least superficially."

"Yes, sir."

"You also know—I have told you—that in my youth there, I was impetuous and headstrong, and that I sometimes showed a pronounced lack of judgment."

"So you have said."

"A half-century ago in Montenegro, Milos Stefanovic and I were relatively close friends, although I never shared his consuming interest in music. We fought together, along with Marko and others in the photograph, for a cause in which we strongly believed. On one occasion in Cetinje, Stefanovic saved my life. And then, for reasons that are now irrelevant, he and I parted, not without rancor. I haven't seen him since that time, and I probably haven't thought about him for twenty years, at least. I mention this by way of telling you that we are faced with an extraordinary circumstance."

"Yes, sir." Although Wolfe's upstairs horsepower is far greater than mine, I've been around long enough to know when he's rationalizing. I stifled a smile.

"I am duty-bound to see this woman." He spread his hands in what for him is a dramatic gesture of helplessness. "I have no choice. Tell her to be here at three o'clock. Also, it's been a long time since Mr. Cohen has joined us for dinner. Call and invite him for tonight.

And tell him we will be serving that cognac he enjoys so much."

I was delighted, of course, that Wolfe had agreed to see Maria. But his wanting Lon Cohen to come for dinner was a bonus. Lon works for the *Gazette,* where he has an office two doors from the publisher's on the twentieth floor. He doesn't have a title I'm aware of, but I can't remember a major story in New York that he didn't know more about than ever appeared in the *Gazette,* or anyplace else, for that matter. Lon and I play in the same weekly poker game, but he only comes to dinner at Wolfe's a couple of times a year, and it's almost always when Wolfe wants information. This is all right with Lon, because he's gotten a fat file of exclusive stories from us through the years, not to mention some three-star meals.

As it turned out, Lon was available, although he wanted to know what was up. I told him he'd just have to wait, and that there was some Remisier to warm his tummy after dinner. He said for that he'd sell any state secrets he had lying around his office. And Maria could make it at three. "Does this mean Mr. Wolfe will take the case?" she asked over the phone breathlessly.

"Who knows?" I answered. "But at least he'll see you, and that alone is progress."

I went to the kitchen to tell Fritz there would be a guest for dinner. "Archie, things are happening today, I can tell. Is he going back to work?"

Fritz always fusses when Wolfe is in one of his periodic relapses. He acts like we're on the brink of bankruptcy at all times and thinks that if Wolfe isn't constantly performing feats of detection, there won't be enough money to pay his salary or, more important, the food bills. Needless to say, the last two years of inactivity by Wolfe had left Fritz with a permanently long puss, and I more than once caught him in the kitchen wringing his hands, looking heavenward, and muttering things in French. "Archie, he needs to work," Fritz would say. "He enjoys his food more then. Work sharpens his appetite." I always replied that his appetite seemed plenty sharp to me, but he just shook his head mournfully.

This time, though, I was delighted to report that prospects were improving. "Keep your carving knives crossed," I told him, "and say a prayer to Brillat-Savarin."

"I'll do more than that," he said. "Tonight, you and Mr. Wolfe and Mr. Cohen will have a dinner to remember." Whistling, he turned to his work, and I whistled a bit myself on the way back to the office.

3

Maria was ten minutes early, and she looked as frightened as she had that morning. She'd changed and was wearing a soft Angora peaches-and-cream-colored number, one of those dresses that seems equally appropriate for daytime wear or for dinner and dancing. I wanted to put my arms around her, but I sat her in the red leather chair instead, and once again arranged the three notes to Stefanovic on Wolfe's desk blotter. Even geniuses need reference material.

Wolfe was in the kitchen with Fritz conferring on dinner: beef tournedos with sauce béarnaise, squash with sour cream and dill, celery-and-cantaloupe salad, and blueberry tart. When I told him Maria had arrived, he grimaced. The idea of having a woman in the house revolts him, and it's all the worse if her presence means he'll have to go to work. I went back to the office, and two minutes later he walked in, detoured around Maria, and dipped his head an eighth of an inch before sitting. That's his version of a bow.

"Madam," he said, "Mr. Goodwin has informed me of your earlier visit. He also told you, correctly, that I am no longer actively practicing as a private investigator. But your uncle—if indeed he is that—is an individual to whom I owe an incalculable debt. That debt alone is sufficient reason for my seeing you.

"Let me forewarn you, however," he said, waggling a finger at her, "that this discussion is not tantamount to a contract."

Maria nodded slowly, but she was frowning. "Mr. Wolfe, you said 'if indeed he is that.' Do you question that I am the niece of—"

Wolfe cut her off, but I can't report what he said because it was in Serbo-Croatian, of which I know maybe fifteen words. He spoke what sounded like two or three sentences, and Maria responded in the same tongue. They went back and forth for about a minute. Then Wolfe nodded and turned to me. "Archie, I asked Miss Radovich several questions that only someone close to Milos Stefanovic could have answered. I am satisfied with her replies. If you want the substance of our conversation, I'll supply it later."

"No problem," I said. "I've been secretly studying Serbo-Croatian on records up in my room for the last eight years, and I've taken down everything you said in shorthand."

Wolfe glared at me and turned back to Maria. "I understand from Mr. Goodwin that your uncle is unaware of your visit. Also, he apparently wants to avoid any revelation of these notes?"

Maria nodded. "Uncle Milos became extremely upset when I suggested he go to the police."

Wolfe's eyes narrowed. "Miss Radovich, who sent these to your uncle?"

"Well, I . . . if I knew, I wouldn't have come to you. That's what I was hoping you would find out."

"Come now," Wolfe said, leaning forward. "Surely you don't take Mr. Goodwin and me for lackwits. You must have some suspicion—a strong one—about who is harassing your uncle. And you want us to either confirm or reject that suspicion. That is why you're here."

"I am here because I want to know who sent those notes, and I want to know how serious the threats in them are to my uncle," Maria answered evenly, returning Wolfe's gaze without blinking. Her fright seemed to have evaporated, although her hands were still clenched tightly in her lap.

Wolfe's shoulders rose and fell a fraction of an inch. "Very well. You told Mr. Goodwin that your uncle had enemies within the orchestra. Let us proceed in that direction."

"I also told Mr. Goodwin that it is not unusual for the conductor of a major orchestra to find strong opposition. Name a famous conductor, and almost surely he has encountered difficulties."

"But *mortal* difficulties?" Wolfe said, raising his eyebrows. "I don't know enough, or care enough, about symphony orchestras to be able to name their conductors, but I can't recall ever hearing of threats on one's life, and mortal threats are implied in these notes. Madam, I cannot fire without powder. Surely you can suggest someone who would benefit from your uncle's departure from the orchestra." He turned a palm over. "A past grudge? A slight? Jealousy? Disagreement over artistic competence?"

"I just can't believe that anyone connected with the Symphony would—"

"You felt these notes warranted a visit to me. Now you have my attention. You seek aid; we can give none without your full cooperation. If you choose to deflect my questions, it is fruitless to continue."

Maria winced. "I'm sorry. Of course you're right." She paused, picking her way. "When my uncle was chosen to be the Symphony's music director, the decision was not popular with everyone. But Jason Remmers—the board chairman of the Symphony—insisted on hiring Uncle Milos. He had talked to him several times in London, and was very persuasive in getting him to move to this country."

"Remmers—of the beer family?" Wolfe asked.

"I'm not sure, but I think perhaps that is right," Maria said.

Wolfe nodded. Remmers is his brand, and has been almost as long as I've known him, which means he's probably consumed a freight-train full at his rate of intake. He used the opportunity to finish the first of two bottles Fritz had brought in. "Who opposed Mr. Remmers's choice?" he asked as he poured the other bottle into his glass.

"Mr. Meyerhoff, the orchestra's managing director, was against Uncle Milos from the start. He felt, or so I've heard, that my uncle is too strict, too demanding."

"And too difficult to get along with?" Wolfe purred.

"Yes, that too. You knew my uncle, Mr. Wolfe; he is a perfectionist. He will not accept anything less than the maximum efforts from his musicians. If he is demanding, it is because he wants the finest possible performance. Mr. Remmers was aware of that when he came to London. Uncle Milos had a reputation there as a firm leader, and the Symphony needed someone firm. But Mr. Meyerhoff and Mr. Hirsch were hostile to him from the start."

"Mr. Hirsch?" Wolfe asked.

"David Hirsch, the associate conductor of the orchestra," Maria said.

"Was Mr. Hirsch associate conductor when Milos Stefanovic joined the orchestra?" Wolfe asked.

"Yes, and that is part of the problem. He is said to have wanted the conductor's job for himself at the time. From the day my uncle arrived in New York, they have had what you would call strained relations, although Mr. Hirsch has always been very pleasant to me. And so has Mr. Meyerhoff, for that matter."

"Have any other members of the orchestra or staff feuded with your uncle?" Wolfe asked.

Maria paused for several seconds before shaking her head. "No . . . other than perhaps the usual resentment of musicians toward a strict conductor. At least none that I've heard of."

"Miss Radovich, does your uncle have close friends in New York? Persons he sees socially?"

Another pause. "Uncle Milos has never made friends easily. He likes to be alone. But there is one *woman* . . ." She came down hard on the last word.

"Yes?" Wolfe prodded.

Maria pursed her lips. "She and Uncle Milos go to the theater often, and to parties. She has him for dinner, and sometimes she comes to our apartment after concerts for a drink or late supper."

"Her name?"

"Lucinda Forrester-Moore. She's a widow, and well-known in society. Her picture is in the newspapers a lot."

No argument there. Lucinda Forrester-Moore's name seemed to pop up in at least one of the columns every few days, and she was a favorite subject for the photographers, too. The *Gazette* picture file on her was probably bulging. Lily Rowan had introduced us a couple of years back, I think at Rusterman's restaurant, and while she has a few too many years on her for my taste, I have to admit that for an older model, she still looks to be in good running condition. Uncle Milos was doing all right.

"Is your uncle's relationship with this woman a romantic one?" Wolfe asked.

"I wish I could say no," Maria answered. "But I think he is . . . very interested. And she is a *hunter*." She hit the arm of the chair with a fist. "She has always chased famous men—she is known for it. But Uncle Milos can't see that. I've tried to tell him—"

"Is this relationship approaching marriage, Miss Radovich?" Wolfe asked.

"Lord, I hope not!" I jumped at the intensity of her answer, and I think it scared Maria herself. She blushed becomingly and cleared her throat before going on. "Uncle Milos has said several times through the years that he has no interest in getting married again."

"Mr. Goodwin mentioned to me that your uncle had been married once years ago," Wolfe said. "Is his former wife alive?"

"Yes. She is a lovely and gracious woman, Mr. Wolfe. She and Uncle Milos were divorced before I was born, and she moved to London."

"Who is she?" Wolfe asked.

"Her name is Alexandra Adjari. I met her for the first time when Uncle Milos and I settled in London and he took the conducting job there. They were not on friendly terms, but she wanted to get to know me."

"She's back to her maiden name," Wolfe said. It wasn't a question.

"Yes, she never remarried. I think she had money of her own, from before she knew Uncle Milos. She has a large flat in Mayfair."

"Just so," said Wolfe. "Have you communicated with her recently?"

"We write at Christmas, but that's all, and I haven't seen her since Uncle Milos and I moved here from London," Maria said.

Wolfe started in on the orchestra again; I'd forgotten how good his technique was when he felt like working, and this was the closest he'd come to working in a long time. He chatted with Maria about orchestras in general, then gradually worked his way to individuals before retreating to generalities again. He repeated this over and over, and I filled at least two dozen notebook pages with the conversation, but these samples will give you the flavor of the entire session:

W: How many musicians does the orchestra have?

M: It varies depending on the particular piece being played, but for a big symphonic number, there are over a hundred onstage, I think.

W: Do they always occupy the same seats?

M: Basically, except for some shuffling around when special instruments are used.

W: Such as?

M: Oh, guitar, glockenspiel, celesta, things like that.

And on another page:

W: Are there women in the orchestra?

M: Oh, yes.

W: How many: Ten? Fifty?

M: I don't know—maybe about fifteen.

W: Has your uncle ever had a particular interest in any one of them?

M: (blushing) No, never. That would be grossly unprofessional, and Uncle Milos is very strict about things like that. He keeps his private life totally separate from his work.

W: How does he feel about liaisons between orchestra members?

M: (blushing again) I really don't know. It's never come up that I'm aware of.

And further on in my notes:

W: Do you know many members of the orchestra well?

M: (pausing) Just a few. I've met some at parties, receptions, things like that.

W: As a group, do you like musicians?

M: I . . . well, it's like anything else; it depends on the individual, some are nice people, some . . . aren't so nice.

W: Do you have an active dislike for anyone in the orchestra?

M: No, I really couldn't say that. No.

W: (leaning forward slightly) What about a particular fondness?

M: (slight pause) I'm pretty busy with my dancing and don't really spend much time around the orchestra or Symphony Hall. When we're not at home, Uncle Milos and I move in separate circles.

And so it went. In all, Wolfe kept at it for almost an hour, and each time he asked her about specific relationships, she tightened up. I could tell when he began to lose interest. The questions got sillier, including one about what kind of clothes women orchestra members wear. About the time I was totally exasperated with him, Wolfe shifted in his chair and said, "Miss Radovich, I have another engagement; Mr. Goodwin knows how to reach you, I believe?"

Maria looked puzzled, nodded, then got up and thanked both of us. Wolfe remained seated as I followed her to the front hall, helped her on with her coat, and assured her I would call her no later than tomorrow.

"But I don't understand; is Mr. Wolfe going to help or not?" she asked.

"I've known him for years, but I don't understand him either, Miss Radovich. It's hell living in the same house with someone who thinks he's an eccentric genius. All I can promise is that I'll call by tomorrow with some kind of news." I opened the door for her and watched her walk down our front steps for the second time that day. When I got back to the office, Wolfe was scowling.

"She's withholding something, of course," he said.

I nodded. "She was too slow in answering a few times."

"She's trying to protect someone," he said. "Someone

she thinks might have written those notes. But she doesn't want to believe it."

"No argument here," I said.

"Your impression?" Wolfe asked. Over the years, he has convinced himself that I'm an expert on women, and I've tried my best to maintain the image. "Seems responsible and levelheaded, despite the nervousness," I said. "And certainly attractive. She probably has a man. I thought you would get into that a little more with her, but maybe you've lost your touch. Could be she's having an affair with someone in the orchestra, which raises all sorts of interesting possibilities."

Wolfe winced. "Talk to her. Take her dancing. Find out whom she's shielding." Having shown he was still capable of giving a direct order, he lifted his bulk out of the chair and headed for the elevator and his afternoon appointment with the orchids.

4

The three of us sat in the office with coffee and brandy, Wolfe and I at our desks and Lon in the red leather chair. Fritz had made good on his promise of a meal to remember: the beef tournedos had never been so good, and the blueberry tart got passed around the table twice. Dinner conversation had ranged from the role of the Palestinians in the Middle East to the future of American cities and the effectiveness of wage-price controls.

Lon passed a hand over his dark slicked-back hair and smiled. "As usual, I've had a splendid evening here, and if anything, the brandy has improved since the last time I had the honor of sampling it. But I know you well enough to realize this isn't strictly social. And tonight, I'm even more curious than in the past, because of your recent . . . inactivity."

"Mr. Cohen, we've been able to help each other on numerous occasions," Wolfe said between sips of coffee. "I'll repeat a question I've asked before: On balance, are we substantially even?"

Lon threw up a hand and laughed. "No complaints. None. As I've said in the past, I'm running ahead on the deal. If I've got an answer that can help in any way, it's yours."

Wolfe nodded. "For reasons I can't divulge now—and which indeed I may never be able to reveal—I need information on the operations and personnel of the New York Symphony Orchestra. Based on my experience with the scope of your knowledge on a variety of subjects, I'm confident you can supply this information."

Lon grinned and took another sip of Remisier. He was being flattered, none too subtly, by the best, and fattest, detective in New York and probably the world, and he didn't mind it a bit.

"I didn't realize you had an interest in orchestral music," he said, scratching his chin. "Well, I guess I know a fair amount about what goes on over at Symphony Hall. And if I don't, we've got a music critic with more pipelines than OPEC. Shoot."

Wolfe rang for beer and readjusted himself. "From what little I've learned about the orchestra, it appears that some tensions exist among its principals, both the performers and the management. Do you know this to be the case?"

"That's a delicate way of putting it," Lon said. "The truth is that the Symphony's been a jungle for several years. There was a string of weak music directors, none of them able to control the orchestra. Then they brought this guy Stevens over from England a couple years ago, and he has a reputation as one tough cookie. But if anything, the situation seems to have gotten worse."

"Is all the bickering a manifestation of artistic temperaments?" Wolfe asked. He had never thought much of highbrow music or the people who made it.

"That's part of it of course," Lon said. "But there's a lot more. For one thing, Charlie Meyerhoff, the managing director, has always resented Jason Remmers—feels he's a dilettante with no real knowledge of music who has his position simply because of wealth and social power."

"Mr. Remmers is the Symphony's board chairman, I believe?"

"Right, he's from the old beer family—that beer," Lon said, pointing to the bottles on Wolfe's desk. "Only he's never been much interested in the beer business, which disappointed his father. Henry Remmers must be close to eighty now, and still has active control of the firm. But Jason, who's about fifty, married society, and his wife has always been big for the arts. She's been in her glory the last few years. Actually, Jason's done a pretty fair job as chairman. It's a nonpaying post, and a big part of the role is fund-raising. He's an outgoing guy, damn popular around town, and he seems to know how to coax money out of the mattresses, because the orchestra's deficit has been cut way down."

"And he is also responsible for Mr. Stevens's move from London?" Wolfe asked.

"Absolutely. As I said, Stevens has a reputation for being tough, a real hard-nose. The Symphony had suffered from a lack of leadership and discipline, or so our music critic felt compelled to write every other Sunday."

"But Mr. Stevens hasn't been the answer?" Wolfe asked.

"Not really," Lon said, pausing for another sip of brandy. "I don't follow the Symphony like I do the Knicks, but I know there's been plenty of offstage backbiting. Both Meyerhoff and David Hirsch, the associate conductor, have been plenty open about their feelings concerning Stevens. They apparently feel—again, this is our music critic talking—that his Prussian approach hasn't worked. Oh, the orchestra has more discipline now, but at the expense of spirit. They're all so damned terrified of Stevens, or so the story goes, that the quality of the playing has fallen off. Now, I'll concede that Meyerhoff and Hirsch both have a hatchet they want to hone: Meyerhoff resents Remmers, and so probably would have criticized anyone he picked. And Hirsch wanted the job himself, from what I've heard, but doesn't have the ability to handle it."

"Is this manner of tension and infighting usual in an orchestra?" Wolfe asked as I refilled Lon's snifter and my own.

"I suppose so, to a degree," Lon answered. "Hirsch didn't get along with the last music director either, and what little I know about Meyerhoff tells me he's not exactly Mr. Sunshine. That artistic temperament you mention is justification for all kinds of behavior in the theater and music world. But the fact remains that Stevens, whatever his musical abilities, has not pulled the orchestra together the way Remmers hoped he would."

Wolfe made a face, probably envisioning wild-eyed musicians swearing at one another and throwing tantrums. He continued questioning Lon, asking about the personnel and mechanics and operation of the Symphony. Lon will always say he doesn't know much about a given subject, but invariably he turns out to be a two-legged encyclopedia on any topic you throw out. The Lon Cohen I know best seems most at home holding a pair and betting the pot, and his knowledge of the orchestra surprised even me. I could see that Wolfe was careful not to appear overly interested in Stevens, but he kept circling back to him.

Finally, at a quarter to one, Lon stretched his arms and allowed as how he had to be bright-eyed for an early-morning meeting with the publisher. "I'd kill to know what you're up to," he said, grinning at Wolfe, "but I know you aren't going to open up, so I'll just hope for the first call if something breaks. And if nothing does, I've still had the kind of evening that makes me forget we're in the midst of one of the most violent cities in the world." Lon lifted his empty glass to Wolfe and rose.

"Mr. Cohen, I appreciate your patience, and I thank you for dining with us," Wolfe said. "One more favor, if you will: Can Mr. Goodwin get access to your back files on the orchestra?"

"Consider it done," Lon said. "Archie, call before you come, and I'll clear it with our morgue." I went with Lon to the door, saw him out, and bolted it for the night, returning to the office, where Wolfe was reclining in his chair, eyes closed and fingers interlaced over his stomach.

"Okay," I said, returning to my desk, "I retract several recent comments; you really do still know how to work. But where are we? What have we got? All we really know is—"

"Archie!" It was well short of a bellow, but it stopped me. "Your notebook. Instructions."

5

Because I function best on at least eight hours' sleep, it was nine-thirty when I rolled out and showered, and almost ten by the time I got to the kitchen. Fritz had my copy of the *Times* propped up on the rack at the small table where I eat, and a steaming pot of coffee was ready, along with wheatcakes and bacon. I nodded to him and attacked the paper, but I could feel his eyes as I read and sipped the coffee. I finally looked up.

"Archie, how was last night?" he asked, kneading his hands. "Was the food all right? Did everything go well?"

"The tournedos were out of this world, your best work. Mr. Cohen praised them at least three times. He said it was the finest meal he'd had in years."

"Archie . . ." Fritz's dark eyes implored. "You know what I am asking you. Is he working again?"

I started in on the wheatcakes before answering. "It's possible. Even probable. I have some instructions, but I'll never be able to concentrate on them unless I can eat in peace." Fritz reddened and quickly turned away to begin working on lunch.

In fact, I did have instructions, but they were slender. Wolfe had said last night he would take the case, but only with the proviso (his word) that Maria Radovich deliver her uncle to the house for a conversation. At that point, I had accused him of trying to dodge work by setting up an impossible requirement, but he insisted that he had to see the potential victim. "Only Mr. Stevens is likely to give us an accurate accounting of who his enemies might be, at least those within the orchestra," Wolfe had said. "It is almost surely a nest of eccentrics, and no one knows them better than he. That his niece can't—or won't—be of much help has become obvious." I was also to go through the *Gazette* files on Stevens and his previous orchestral jobs and find any other information the clips might contain.

It was ten-thirty when I went to the office, opened the morning mail, and tried to call Maria with the mixed news that Wolfe would take the case—if she could deliver Uncle Milos to West Thirty-fifth Street. No answer. She was probably at a dance rehearsal, and Stevens was in his office at Symphony Hall, I supposed. I then called Lon and had better luck. He was through with his meeting and said to come on over.

"I'm still sated from last night," Lon said when I got to his office on the twentieth floor. "Please send my regards again to Fritz. Now for business: our librarian knows you're coming down to go through some clips. You can't take anything out of the morgue—house rules. But there's a photocopying machine right there. And, Archie, if something big is about to happen at the Symphony, don't forget your friends."

Ten minutes later, I was set up in the corner of a high-ceilinged dingy room with a stack of envelopes labeled "NY Symphony," one fat envelope per year, plus another, thinner envelope that read: "Stevens, Milan, NY Symph. Conduc., 1975–date."

There wasn't much in the clips that we hadn't already learned from Maria or Lon, but I was interested in the biography of Stevens that ran just after his appointment. It called him a "Yugoslav by birth" and gave his original name. It was mostly basic material: marriage and divorce, previous positions, awards, and a brief mention that his niece would be living with him in New York. The few direct quotes were general ones where he said things like "The New York Symphony is one of the world's great orchestras" and "I'm overwhelmed by the appointment." I made a photocopy of the biography, along with one of a particularly negative concert review the *Gazette* critic had done last year calling Stevens "unimaginative in his selections of music, uninspired in his leadership, and unimpressive at the podium."

Wolfe was at his desk reading and drinking beer when I walked in at five minutes to one. "There's not a lot to report," I said, replying to his questioning glance. "I've been to the *Gazette* and have some clips on Stevens." I laid them on his blotter. "Nothing exciting, except that their biography includes his given name, which must have eluded at least a few of their nine hundred thousand readers."

Wolfe wouldn't give me the satisfaction of a scowl. He spread the photocopies on his desk and began reading. After two minutes, he looked up. "Has he agreed to come?"

"I haven't gotten to Maria, or anybody else at home," I said, turning again to the phone. "I'll try again now."

"Later, after lunch," he said, hauling his bulk out of the chair and making for the dining room.

I'm sure Fritz's potato pancakes were superb, but for the second time in two days, my taste buds were on automatic pilot. When we were back·in the office with coffee, I made another call to the Stevens-Radovich apartment. There was an answer this time, but not what I wanted. The maid said Maria wasn't expected home until late that night, so I left a message for her to call me—whenever she got in. "We can try going directly to Stevens," I suggested. "He's probably over at Symphony Hall right now."

Wolfe slowly set his book down, dog-earing a page. "No, Archie, our commitment is to Miss Radovich, not Mr. Stevens. Any communication with her uncle must be done through her, or with her approval."

I swiveled around, ready to argue, but the book was open and in front of his face again. After five minutes of thinking dark thoughts, I got up noisily and went to the hall, grabbing my coat from the rack and slamming the front door behind me. A light rain had begun, blending with my mood. I pulled up my collar and headed east, cooling off as I went. I was being unfair to Wolfe, I argued with myself. After all, he had agreed to take the case, although on one condition. And it was obviously going to be up to me to fulfill that condition. I turned north on Eighth Avenue and ducked into a diner where I sometimes stop for coffee. This time I ordered milk from the counterman, who had only one other customer, an old guy about six stools down who was hunched over a bowl of chili.

I took a few sips of the milk and went to the pay phone to look up the number of Maria's dance troupe, which had its studio on Forty-sixth Street in the theater district. I dialed and got a female voice, along with music in the background.

"Yes, Miss Radovich is here," the voice said, "but she's in the middle of a rehearsal right now. They should be taking a break in a few minutes." I left my name and gave her the pay-phone number. I was on the third glass of milk, with a slice of peach pie thrown in, when the phone rang. "Mr. Goodwin?" Her voice was still breathless, although this time it could have been from the dancing.

After I assured her it was me despite the different phone number, the questions started tumbling out.

"Hold it," I said. "Now catch your breath and listen while I fill you in. Mr. Wolfe says yes, he'll take your money and try to solve the problem. But you've got to do something for us."

"Yes, what is it?"

"Miss Radovich, you've got to persuade your uncle to come to Mr. Wolfe's house for a talk."

Several seconds passed, and when she spoke, she sounded desperate. "You know he won't do that—I couldn't get him to."

"Look, Miss Radovich, when you first called, I wouldn't have given a Canadian dime for our chances of waking up Mr. Wolfe. I'm happy to say I was wrong. Now he's awake, but he's also stubborn, very stubborn. He wants to see Milan Stevens in his office. Now, if you don't think you can pull it off, I'll be glad to come over, and we can talk to him together."

"No!" she replied in something between a whisper and a shout. "If you came, he would be horribly angry both with you and with me. I must get back to rehearsal now, and we practice again after dinner, so I won't be home until late, almost midnight. But then I will ask Uncle Milos. I promise you." I repeated that I'd be happy to be there for moral support, but that only rattled her more. I gave up and said I'd wait to hear.

The rain had stopped, and I needed exercise, so I walked. By the time I got home, it was a little after four, which put Wolfe in the plant rooms and meant I probably wouldn't see him again that day: I was taking Lily to the Rangers game after an early supper at Rusterman's.

If I ever decide to spend the rest of my life with one woman—a less-than-even bet—that woman will be Lily Rowan. That is, if she ever decides to spend the rest of her life with one man, and you'll have to ask her about the odds on that yourself. All of which may give you some idea about our relationship.

Lily's late father came over from Ireland and discovered that New York could use some new sewers, so he spent a lifetime building them and getting rich and powerful in the process and determining who should be elected to what office in the city and the state and sometimes Congress. Today, Lily lives in a penthouse just off Park Avenue, and at least one of her French Impressionist paintings has curators at four museums drooling.

This is fine, but more important to me are dark blue eyes and hair just a shade darker than cornsilk and the best-looking legs between Paris and Chicago, legs that are not only great to ogle, but which also move around a dance floor better than any others I've ever been with. Not to mention that each of us seems to have the other measured pretty well all the time, so nobody worries about playing parts or faking emotions.

"Escamillo, my love," Lily said over coffee after dinner, "methinks your mind is a long way from Irish colleens and hockey games. No, don't try to deny it," she said, reaching across to squeeze my arm. "Maybe it's intuition or whatever those women's magazines have taken to calling it these days, but all the way down to my toes, I have a feeling that Nero Wolfe's back at work. Or maybe it's because you've scratched your right cheek just below the ear at least four times tonight, which only happens when you're nervous, and you're only nervous when you're on a case. Of course I'd kill to know all about it, but you know damn well I'm not going to ask."

I grinned and leaned across the booth to kiss Lily's cheek—just below the right ear. "Now I see why you do so well against me when we play poker," I said. "I suppose you're going to tell me I rub my chin when I pair up or that my left eye twitches when I fill a straight?" She answered with a wink.

True to her word, Lily didn't bring up the subject of Wolfe again, and I made sure my right hand stayed away from my face. The Rangers beat Boston six-five on a short-handed goal with less than three minutes to play. We cheered as loudly as any of the seventeen thousand others in the Garden, but our enthusiasm dissolved into awkward silence as soon as we were outside.

"I'm aware," Lily said after we'd gotten a cab, "that you're a million miles away right now. I was planning to ask you in for a brandy, but if you want to take a rain check, that's fine. It wouldn't hurt me to get to bed at a decent hour for a change."

"You know of course that your knack of saying and doing precisely the right thing at the right time makes you totally irresistible to me," I said.

"Of course I know it. I've bought a table for a benefit at the Churchill two weeks from tonight, and I expect you to be my consort."

"Consider it done," I said as we pulled up to her building. I went as far as the lobby with her, and we kissed while the hallman tactfully kept his head buried in a paperback. "Take care, Escamillo," she said, easing out of my grasp and planting the tip of her finger on my nose. "I want to hear all about what you and Wolfe are up to—when you're ready to talk about it."

Back in the cab, I gave the driver a Forty-sixth Street address. About halfway through the hockey game, I'd made up my mind to try to catch Maria at her rehearsal and take her home. On the way, I hoped, I could talk her into introducing me to Uncle Milos.

My watch said eleven-fifteen when the cabbie slid to the curb in front of a brick building on a dark stretch a half-block east of Broadway. There was a stationery store at street level, with a doorway on one side with a sign above it that said "Elmar Dance Company, 2nd Floor." I walked up a long, creaky stairway, moving toward a light at the top and the sounds of what I assumed must be dance music. The stairs ended at a small reception area with a desk and a lumpy couch and dusty photographs of dancers hanging at cockeyed angles on the walls. A hallway led farther back, to where the music was coming from.

Just as I started in the direction of the sound, a tall blonde with lots of eye makeup and an overnight case popped out of a doorway about halfway down, obviously on her way out.

"Hi, who you lookin' for?" she asked, showing a mouthful of teeth that deserved to be in a chewing-gum ad. When I answered, she said Maria was changing. "Why don't you take a seat? She's got to pass you to get out of here."

Three more dancers, two of them lookers, sailed by chattering before Maria came out, wearing slacks and with her hair tied back in a scarf. She saw me and stopped, but before she could say anything, I was up and smiling.

"The more I thought about it, the more I felt I should take you home tonight. Come on, we can get a cab over on Broadway. And on the way, I'll tell you why we should see your uncle together."

Maria frowned and shook her head. "No, I've told you he won't talk to you when he finds out why you've come. Please, I promised on the telephone that I'd ask him tonight about seeing Mr. Wolfe."

Walking to Broadway and then on the cab ride north, I kept pressing Maria, but whatever charm Wolfe thinks I have with women wasn't working on this one. Her one concession was to let me come into the building with her, but only as far as the lobby. I would wait there while she went up to talk to her uncle. Then, if she needed reinforcements, she'd call down for me. I wasn't wild about the plan, because Stefanovic didn't sound like the type to let his niece talk him into a damn thing. But I wasn't getting a choice.

The cab squealed to a stop in front of an undistinguished brick building in the first block east of Park. I was expecting a little more class, at least a doorman, but this place looked like dozens of other fifty-year-old buildings in the area. I paid the driver, and we went into a small, dimly lit lobby. "Tom, this is Mr. Goodwin; he's going to wait for me here," Maria said to the hallman, a young, weak-chinned guy who looked up from behind the counter and nodded. "I'll come down or call down for him in a few minutes."

I hope so, I thought as she went up in the elevator. I plopped down on one of the dark red sofas and started thumbing through a magazine that was on the coffee table. No more than two minutes had passed when the phone at the front desk rang. "Mr. Goodwin, Miss Radovich wants you to go on up," Tom said. "It's the ninth floor, the door to your right as you get off the elevator. You can't miss it; there're only two apartments to the floor."

Either Uncle Milos wasn't home or Maria had gotten some fast results one way or the other. Ready for the worst, I tried to prepare an approach to him as the automatic elevator growled its way up to nine. But I wasn't prepared for what I saw when the doors opened.

Maria was standing in the doorway of the apartment, or more correctly, leaning against one side of it. Her eyes were open wide, but she barely acknowledged me. I put an arm around her for support as her legs began to fold up. "On the floor . . ." she said, covering her face with her hands. "Dead, dead, dead . . ."

6

I got Maria inside and shut the door. We were in an entrance hall that had a chandelier and a handsome Oriental rug. I led her to a chair and eased her down as the sobs started. "Where?" I asked. She pointed to an open door at the far end of the hall. "Stay here," I said. "Don't try to move."

The doorway led into a good-sized library with a high ceiling, fireplace, dark paneling, lots of bookshelves, a grand piano, and another Oriental rug, a Kashan. The body was lying facedown on the rug in one corner near a high monk-style writing desk that had a stool behind it. I knelt and made a quick check, but Maria had been right. Milan Stevens was dead, and it wasn't hard to figure out why: The back of his white shirt was torn and stained dark red, and a fancy long-handled letter opener, one of those made to look like a sword, lay a few feet away. The blood on the opener glistened in the light, and from the look of Stevens's shirt, that little sword had been run in and out of him several times.

I tried to freeze the scene in my mind, but there wasn't much to freeze. None of the furniture appeared out of place, and there was no indication of a struggle. A softcover book lay open on the monk's desk, and I covered my hand with my handkerchief as I turned the pages. It was music, plus a lot of penciled notations that might as well have been in Urdu. For the record, the cover sheet of the music said "Symphony No. 4 in E minor, for Orchestra, by Johannes Brahms, Op. 98."

I went back to the hall, where Maria was still sitting. She'd stopped crying and now was staring straight ahead. "He is dead, isn't he?" she asked, blinking.

"Yes. Now listen carefully; I'm going to have to call the police, and I have to do it soon. When they come, tell them everything about the notes, about going to see Mr. Wolfe, all of it. But first, I have two things to do. Please stay right here." She nodded, but otherwise there was no reaction or expression. Shock was settling in.

I went back to the study and, using the handkerchief again, dialed the number I know best. Wolfe answered after one ring.

"The notes must have been for real," I said. "Stevens is dead. Stabbed in his study. I'm there now, with Maria, and I'm about to call the police. Instructions?"

I could hear him draw in air and let it out slowly. "No," he said. "I suppose you'll have to go to headquarters?"

"Without question," I said. "And I've told Maria not to keep anything from them. I figure it's going to be a long night. I'll report first thing in the morning, if they let me out by then."

"Very well," Wolfe said with disgust. "Have you eaten?" I assured him that Rusterman's lamb chops would carry me through the night, and I went back to Maria. She hadn't moved and gave me another mechanical nod when I told her I was going to the lobby for a couple of minutes.

Tom was still behind the counter. "Excuse me," I said with what I hoped was a friendly smile. "Did Mr. Stevens have any guests earlier this evening, before Miss Radovich and I got here?"

He looked up with a slightly amused expression. "Why don't you ask him yourself?"

"He's asleep," I said. "And Miss Radovich had been expecting a visitor. She wondered if anyone had come by."

Tom was sizing me up, trying to decide whether or not I was okay, and he finally made up his mind. "Well . . . there was one," he said. "His name was Milner, or something like that. He came in about eight-fifteen, but didn't stay long—maybe five minutes."

"His first name?" I asked.

"Didn't leave one. I just called upstairs to Mr. Stevens and told him Mr. Milner was here, and he said to send him up."

"Did Mr. Milner say anything to you when he left?"

"Nope. Just walked on out. All I saw was his back going through the lobby."

"And he was the only caller?"

"Yeah."

"Thanks, Tom," I said. "You've leveled with me, and now I'd better tell you something. Mr. Stevens is dead—killed. The police will be here soon."

I watched his face closely, and got the predictable openmouthed, wide-eyed look. "What? Hey, why didn't you say that right away?" He jumped up, knocking his chair over. He looked scared. "I can't tell them anything," he said, swallowing hard. "It must have been that Milner guy, huh? What should I do when they come?"

"Take it easy," I said. "They'll want to know just what you told me. About Mr. Milner, about anything else that might have happened tonight that was unusual. Was there anything?"

He swallowed again and shook his head. "No . . . a real quiet night. Nothing at all."

"Okay, Tom. One other thing: Have you ever seen Mr. Milner here before?"

He paused and screwed up his face. "I think so, maybe with Miss Radovich. But I'm not positive—I wouldn't want to say for sure."

I said thanks again, and left him at his post to sweat out the cops' arrival. But they weren't going to come until somebody called them, which I now had to do fast. When I got back upstairs, I found Maria still in the chair, zombielike. I squeezed her arm lightly and went to the study to dial Homicide South.

"My name is Goodwin," I told the voice that answered. "I'm reporting a murder." I gave the address and floor, but the guy wanted more details and my full name. "Just send somebody, and they can get it all firsthand," I said, hanging up.

It would be five, maybe ten minutes before we got company. I checked on Maria again. "The police will be here soon," I said. "Are you all right?"

Her face was colorless, and she was shaking. I got her to tell me where the sherry was, and I filled a glass. A few sips seemed to help; she inhaled deeply and attempted a smile.

I knelt on one knee next to her chair. "I'll take a fast look around the rest of the place before they get here, if you don't mind. But first—do you know someone named Milner?"

It was as if I'd slapped her. "Jerry. What . . . how do you know him? How . . ." She started to get up, but I had my hand on her shoulder.

"He was here earlier tonight," I said. "That guy at the desk just told me. He also said he thought he'd seen him here before—with you."

Maria brushed her hair back from her face. "Yes, Jerry and I . . . we know each other. He's a violinist with the orchestra. But I don't see why he would have come here tonight. He knew I would be in rehearsals until at least . . ." The words trailed off, and she made a face. "Oh, no, *no,* he could never . . . no . . ." She closed her eyes tight and kept shaking her head until I squeezed her shoulder.

"How did he and your uncle get along?"

Maria took a deep breath. "They had very different personalities. There were some arguments, but nothing that would, that . . ." She turned her palms up and made a gesture of helplessness.

"Were the arguments because of you, Maria?"

She nodded, and the sobs started again. I squeezed her hands and told her to stay put while I prowled.

The place wasn't luxurious, but it had a solid, substantial feel to it. The rooms were big and well-furnished. The cost of the Oriental rugs alone had to be more than most people spend on all their furnishings in a lifetime, and the paintings included a Cézanne on the living room wall that Lily would covet.

Nothing seemed to have been disturbed anywhere. A jewelry box on the dressing table in Maria's room was stuffed with things that any self-respecting thief would have taken, and gold cufflinks lay on top of the dresser in her uncle's bedroom.

The apartment had about eight rooms, and I was just finishing my quick tour of them when the doorbell rang. It was two plainclothes detectives and a uniformed cop. I recognized one of the dicks, a guy named Henderson I had met once or twice. He was Central Casting's idea of what a detective should look like: tall, wavy-haired, square-jawed, and wearing a white trench coat with hardware all over it. But he was also solid, and had a good reputation in the department.

He gave a tight-lipped smile when he saw me. "I'll be

damned, they said a guy named Goodwin had phoned in, but I figured it couldn't be you, what with Wolfe on the shelf these days."

I smiled back. "Goes to show you can't take anything for granted anymore. Have you talked to the hallman yet?"

"I left Mills with him and came straight up. What's the story?"

"The dead man is Milan Stevens, the conductor of the Symphony. He's in there," I said. "This is his niece, Maria Radovich."

Henderson was momentarily jolted by the news, but quickly recovered and switched on the standard we're-here-to-help manner for Maria, who stood. "Please sit down, Miss Radovich. You can stay right here for now, but we'll want to talk to you later, just for a short time." I followed Henderson into the study, where his partner and the uniformed man were bending over the body.

"Christ, this guy was big stuff, wasn't he?" Henderson whispered to me. "This may get Cramer and the commissioner out of bed."

"Looks like he's been carved up pretty good," the other detective said. "Apparently with that letter opener."

Henderson nodded. "Ed, phone for the M.E.," he said to the uniform. "Use a handkerchief. Okay, Goodwin, fill me in. How'd you happen to be here?"

I knew I would have to repeat the story several times before dawn, but I gave it all to him, and he made a few notes as I talked.

"And you say Wolfe has those letters to Stevens at home?" he asked when I was done.

I nodded, and Henderson looked around the library. The impact this case would have in the department and around town was just beginning to hit him, and he was measuring his moves. "Goodwin, you'd better come downtown with us later. Right now, I want to talk to her."

Henderson led Maria into the living room while I stayed and watched the other two combing the study and taking notes. A while later the medical examiner came puffing in with his little black bag, followed by a police photographer. "At least three, maybe four wounds," the doctor said after a quick check. "I'd say for starters that he's been dead more than three hours." My watch read eleven-thirty-five, which didn't make things very rosy for Maria's friend Jerry Milner.

The next few hours are best summarized. Maria had to look at the body once more to satisfy the police, and I went downtown, where my least-favorite member of New York's finest, one Lieutenant George Rowcliff of Homicide, was on duty. He decided to let Inspector Cramer and the commissioner keep snoring so that he could personally handle my interrogation. Over the years, Rowcliff and I have had a relationship that ranges from distaste to outright hatred, but that night made all our previous encounters seem amiable by comparison. Rowcliff has been burned by Wolfe a few times, and he'd never pass a chance to get us into the stew pot. Around headquarters, it was said that he had two goals: to lift Wolfe's and my licenses, and to make captain—in that order. So far he'd struck out at both, although he came pretty close to the former on the Orrie Cather episode.

"Well, well, well, Goodwin," he said when we were alone in a dismal office. "I've been telling the inspector for months that we hadn't heard the last of you and that fat egomaniac. He was sure Wolfe had retired, but I knew there was no way you guys could resist publicity forever. And now you're really in it—up to your necks."

"Egomaniac? Very good, Rowcliff. You've learned a new word. Mr. Wolfe will be so proud of you. I wasn't aware you knew any with more than two syllables. But can you spell it?"

"Listen, you half-assed smartmouth, this time I'm

going to . . ." Rowcliff's eyes were bulging, which always happens when he loses his temper, and he had to
stop talking because if he'd kept on, the stuttering
would have started, too. He took a few breaths, then
started in with the questioning. It went on, with an
occasional assist from a few of his lackeys, for more
than two hours. Rowcliff could be very thorough when
he put his mind to it. In fact, he asked some of the
questions over and over, but I always answered precisely
the same way.

"Let me understand this," he said for about the fourth
time. "You're telling me that the Radovich woman came
to you because Stevens had known Wolfe years ago in
Europe?"

"That's what I'm telling you, Lieutenant. That's what
she told me."

"And that you have three notes in your safe at home
that threatened Stevens's life, notes that you didn't see
fit to turn over to the police at the time?"

"That's what I've said."

"And that Miss Radovich hired you to find out who
wrote those notes? What a fine job you great master-
minds did on this. You realize, Goodwin, that if you'd
come to us with this, Milan Stevens would be alive?"

I stuffed my hands in my pockets and admired the
peeling paint on the ceiling. "Lieutenant, it's brought
back memories, chatting with you tonight, but I get
the feeling that you're running out of questions. Can't
we get a stenographer in here so I can make a statement?"

"Dammit, Goodwin, *I'll* decide when to call the steno!"
Rowcliff screamed. "I could have you locked up as an
accessory."

He couldn't, and we both knew it, but he needed to
let off steam, and I needed a pillow and mattress. I
could tell I was tired when Rowcliff started stuttering
and it didn't even matter to me. I assumed that by this
time Milner had been found and was somewhere in the

building, and I was surprised that Rowcliff hadn't abandoned me to work on him.

Finally, around two-fifteen, he decided I was no longer worth the effort, and a steno came in for my statement. Twenty minutes later, I was on my way home in a patrol car with a sergeant named Foley who didn't like Rowcliff any more than I did, and who had let me hitch a ride north with him. It was three o'clock when I fell into bed and set the alarm for four hours later.

7

No matter how often I see Wolfe propped up in bed, I'm never quite prepared for the sight. Maybe it's his bright yellow pajamas, or the silk coverlet, or the uncertainty as to where he ends and the bed begins, but in that setting he always looks larger than usual, which is saying a lot. I got to his room just after eight, right behind Fritz and his tray with orange juice, hot chocolate, peaches with cream, link sausage, shirred eggs, and whole-wheat toast with currant jam. My alarm clock had kicked me out of bed at seven, and after a shave and shower, I went down to the kitchen for a quick breakfast of my own so I could fill Wolfe in before his morning visit to the plants. He forbids business talk in the dining room, but on rare occasions tolerates it with his breakfast.

"Last night was every bit as delightful as I thought it would be," I said as he started in on the peaches. "Who do you suppose was on duty at Twenty-first Street when I got there?"

"Not Lieutenant Rowcliff?" Wolfe made a face, as he always does when he pronounces the name. He's never forgiven Rowcliff for the time years ago when he searched the brownstone.

"You got it. We exchanged the usual pleasantries, but then, I'm getting ahead of myself. I assume you want it all?"

Wolfe nodded. That meant a verbatim report on the evening, which was no strain. On past occasions, I've repeated hours of word-for-word dialogue to him, and I'd match myself against a tape recorder.

I started with the call to Maria at the dance studio and covered all the rest, right through to Rowcliff's final rantings and my ride home. Wolfe interrupted three or four times with questions, but otherwise concentrated on his tray. As I finished, he drained the last of his chocolate and scowled. "I suppose the police have Mr. Milner by now. What do the papers say?" He gestured to the copies of the *Times* and *Daily News* that Fritz had brought up. I'd read my own copies already.

"There's nothing about Stevens in these editions," I said. "They probably got the story too late. But the afternoons figure to play it big, and you can be sure Lon will be calling soon. Ditto the reporters for the other papers and the TV stations. And I've got a sawbuck that says Cramer punches our doorbell before noon."

"Your money is safe," Wolfe said. "If Mr. Milner is the murderer, Mr. Cramer's army of men will likely have no trouble establishing it. If that's the case, we'll owe Miss Radovich a refund, along with our condolences. Let us for the moment turn our back on the obvious, however. What is your judgment of her?"

"You mean, could she have done it? Absolutely not. Two hundred to one against, at least. She doted on the old man, and besides, she apparently was at the dance studio all afternoon and evening. But that's one that can be checked easily enough."

"Very well," Wolfe said. "I concur that we will almost surely hear from both Mr. Cohen and Mr. Cramer this morning, one with questions, the other with harangues." He leaned back against the pillows and closed his eyes.

"Is that it?" I asked after a half-minute of silence. "Someone you've known for years was killed last night, not more than four miles from here, and I get the feeling that I'm keeping you awake. I'm impressed with the way you're able to conceal your fury."

He looked at me with wide eyes. "Archie, outrage is among your more churlish emotions. If I may contradict you, Mr. Stevens is someone I have *not* known for years. Further—and I realize this is troubling you—I reject summarily any suggestion that Mr. Stevens's death could have been prevented by our turning those notes over to the police. As you've heard me say before, if one person is determined to kill another, it is virtually impossible to prevent the act, short of destroying the potential murderer himself. And whoever dispatched Milan Stevens had in all likelihood made his or her decision long before last night."

Wolfe then opened the *Times,* which signaled the end of the discussion. For the second time in two days, I wanted to slam a door behind me, but decided it was wasted energy. I walked down one flight to the office and found my desk covered with messages that Fritz had taken. One was from Lon, of course, and others from the *Times, Daily News, Post,* and three television stations. I dialed a number, and Lon answered on the first ring.

"All right, Archie, this one's really got us spinning. What gives with Wolfe and Stevens? Naturally, we haven't told the police about your wanting those clips, but I suppose I could always call Cramer and . . ."

"Threats will get you nowhere with a tough gumshoe," I said. "Besides, you could no more snitch on a friend than you could quit the paper for a job in TV. What've you heard about the Stevens thing?"

"What have *I* heard? Why the hell do you think I'm calling you? Nero Wolfe invites me to dinner, ostensibly for a social evening, although I know better. I get pumped about the Symphony in general and Milan Stevens in particular. Then you come to the paper to see our files on the man and the orchestra, and within twelve hours he's killed. And for frosting, I have to read in the final edition of this morning's *Daily News* that Stevens had known Nero Wolfe a million years ago in Yugoslavia, and that Stevens's niece had come to you for help regarding some threatening letters he got. And then"—Lon paused for breath—"our leader storms into my office waving the *News* story and screaming 'I thought *you* were supposed to be the one who's in thick with Wolfe and that sidekick of his, what's-his-name!' "

"You're making up the 'what's-his-name' part," I said, trying to sound offended. "I haven't seen the *News* article yet; it wasn't in the edition we got delivered. But if they quoted Wolfe or me, they made it up." I pawed through the phone messages on my desk. "Let's see, the *News* did call here, at six-fifty this morning, and Fritz answered, but I haven't returned their call. You're the only member of the fourth estate that I've talked to."

"No, they didn't quote you, and apparently they couldn't get to the niece, either. We think that cretin Rowcliff fed them the stuff about Wolfe, and also said you were there when the body was discovered. Give me something, for God's sake. We need a strong lead for our street edition, and besides, my image is hurting with the man who signs my paychecks."

"What does the *News* say about a suspect?" I asked.

"They're questioning a guy," Lon answered. "Named Milner. A violinist with the Symphony. The hallman says he was the last visitor Stevens had before his body was found."

"Look, I probably can't give you much more than Rowcliff shoveled to the *News*," I said. "You can print the fact that Maria Radovich is our client and that we're investigating the case. And if you like, I can give you a pretty good description of the apartment and the way it looked when I first saw Stevens lying there. Other than that, there's not much we can say without an okay from our client. Speaking of which, I've got to call her."

"You probably won't get through," Lon said. "One of our guys has been trying to reach her for the last hour, and the line's busy. Phone's likely off the hook."

Lon took down my description of the apartment, and a few other tidbits I felt I could safely toss in, and I promised him I wouldn't return any other calls from the media for at least an hour.

Lon was right about Maria. I called several times, and the line was always busy. I also kept my word and didn't talk to reporters who phoned during the next hour. Fritz answered on the kitchen extension and gave them all the same message: I was out, and so was Wolfe. When I finally did get around to calling people back, nobody got more than bare bones from me.

After the flurry of calls both in and out, I had some time to open the mail and work briefly on the germination records, although Fritz ran in every five minutes to pump me about the case or ask if I thought Wolfe was getting enough to eat.

The phone hadn't rung for a while, and I'd just gotten another busy signal from Maria's number when I heard the hum of the elevator. At eleven sharp, Wolfe came in with Ondontoglossums for the vase, but because we'd talked earlier, he didn't bother to ask how I'd slept, which was fine with me—I was still irked about his boredom act upstairs.

After he got settled in his chair and rang for beer, I swiveled to face him. "The late edition of the *Daily News* has the murder; Rowcliff talked to them, Lon says, and we're both mentioned. I gave Lon a little color, but just sneezed at the other papers and the television stations. And I've been trying to call Maria for the last hour, but the line's busy."

Fritz came in with two bottles of beer and a glass on a tray. As he set it down in front of Wolfe, the doorbell rang.

It was eleven-oh-six—I made a point of checking my watch, for the record. Wolfe and I looked at each other, and I went to the door, but I knew before I got there who'd be on the other side of the one-way glass. Still, it was comforting when I actually saw the florid, angry face of one Inspector Lionel T. Cramer of Homicide South.

"Come in, Inspector," I said, grinning. "Believe it or not, we were talking about you just this morning, trying to recall when you visited us last. Mr. Wolfe and I have both felt terribly neglected . . ."

I stopped because he ignored me, bolting through to the office with his coat still on. He headed straight for the red leather chair and sat, pulling out a cigar and jamming it unlit into his mouth.

"So help me God, I never thought I'd be in this room again," he snarled at Wolfe. "I honestly thought I'd seen the last of you and this place."

"It has been a long time," Wolfe said. "I seem to recall that on your last visit, you complimented me on what a good working room this is, and you also gave the globe a spin. Will you join me for a beer?"

"No, goddammit, I won't," Cramer said, glancing at the big Gouchard globe in the corner. He looked about the same as the last time I'd seen him a couple of years before, his hair just as gray and rumpled and maybe with another inch added to an already thick midsection. But he still moved fast for a big man and his eyes hadn't lost any of their sharpness. Despite all their battles through the years, he and Wolfe held a grudging respect for each other.

"Mr. Cramer represents the best of the law officer," Wolfe once told me in a rare burst of praise. "It's true that he's impulsive and has a quick temper, but beyond that—and more important—he's honest to a fault, brave, dedicated, and fiercely proud of the New York Police Department. He hates malingerers and incompetents within its ranks and lives with the constant fear that he may someday be responsible for the conviction of an innocent person." Enough of praise. Right now, Cramer was exhibiting the temper segment of his personality.

"You know why I've come," he snarled at Wolfe, chewing on his stogie. "I should have known better than to believe that you and Goodwin had really hung it up. It's been too peaceful the last year or two, and now we've got one of the biggest murders in this town's history, and I'm back here again.

"I really thought the Cather thing finished you," Cramer went on, leaning forward in his chair. "I never asked you how it felt to have a killer working for—"

"Mr. Cramer!" Wolfe spat the words out and brought the palm of his hand down hard on the desk, causing both Cramer and me to jump. "Have I ever taken you to task for the malfeasants who have been employed by the police—some of them in Homicide? Did I ask you how it felt when one of your own lieutenants murdered his wife and children and then shot himself to death? Archie"—he turned to me—"how many operatives have we employed through the years?"

"Four or five, on any regular basis, and another fifteen or twenty on occasions, I suppose. I could look it up."

Wolfe shook his head. "These men, with the single exception of Mr. Cather, consistently conducted themselves with an admirable degree of honor, dignity, and courage, and one was himself killed while in my employ," Wolfe said. He was referring to Johnny Keems, who was run down by a car on a case years ago. "Am I now to be held accountable for the actions of one among all those I have paid through the years? Really, Mr. Cramer." Wolfe was laying it on thick.

"Okay, don't get so testy," Cramer said, his face beet red. "That's ancient history anyway. What I'm really here about—and you know it—is the Milan Stevens murder."

"We were expecting you," Wolfe said. "And you have our attention."

"Well, I'm certainly glad of *that*," Cramer said. "You know that I could lift your licenses again for the withholding of evidence from the police. I've come for those notes. If you'd turned them over to us right away instead of playing cute, Stevens would still be alive."

"Come now, Mr. Cramer," Wolfe said, turning a palm over. "Let us assume for a moment that we had given you those notes after Miss Radovich had left them with me. Can you honestly say they would have caused you to begin a full-scale search for a potential murderer? Or, as I suspect is more likely, would you have dismissed them as the work of a crackpot? And even if you had undertaken a hunt, where would it have ended?"

"At the same place we are now," said Cramer. "With Gerald Milner in custody."

"Indeed?" said Wolfe, raising his eyebrows. "Has Mr. Milner been charged with murder?"

"You know damn well he has," Cramer said, almost shouting. "We picked him up early this morning."

"Has he confessed?" Wolfe asked.

"No, but he's rattled to the point where I think he'll crack sometime today. The hallman in Stevens's building saw him go up, and we found his prints in the apartment. No question, he's it. Now, those notes."

"Certainly. Archie, please get them from the safe and give them to Mr. Cramer. Well, it appears that your case is over very quickly, and I congratulate you. Have you established a motive?"

"Hell, yes," Cramer said as I handed him an envelope with the notes in it. "We've already talked to several orchestra members who heard Stevens screaming at Milner after a rehearsal several weeks ago. It seems that Milner wanted to marry Stevens's niece, but when the old man found out about it, he was furious, didn't think Milner was worthy of her. After that, he singled Milner out during rehearsals, chewing him out, and trying to make him look bad in front of everyone."

"And what does Mr. Milner say about last night?" Wolfe asked.

"He claims Stevens wrote him a note asking him to come to his apartment. Milner says he thought it was to talk about Maria. When he got off the elevator, or so he says, the door to the apartment was open. He called out Stevens's name, and when there was no answer, he went in and found Stevens lying dead on the floor in the library.

"He claims he panicked," Cramer said. "His story is that he ran out, not bothering to close the door, and walked the streets for hours, trying to decide what to do. Our men were at his apartment in Queens waiting for him when he got there at about one-thirty."

Wolfe nodded. "They probably brought him in while Lieutenant Rowcliff was still questioning Mr. Goodwin."

Cramer spat an obscenity. "And he wonders why he hasn't made captain. One of the biggest names in town is murdered, and that idiot decides to handle it all by himself. Not that Goodwin doesn't deserve a two-hour grilling, and more, but the time Rowcliff wasted on him, when he should have been . . . Aw, the hell with it. Quote me, and I'll deny I ever said any of that. Anyway, I'm glad this one's going to be over quick. The heat would've been murder, with the mayor kicking the commissioner, the commissioner kicking everybody in the department, and the papers going nuts over it."

"Again, I congratulate you," Wolfe said.

"Yeah, thanks. No great help to you, though. Maybe this really will be my last time in this office." Cramer stood up and looked around.

"I honestly hope not," Wolfe said. "I always enjoy your visits."

"That's more than I can say," Cramer answered. "Well . . ." He was staring at the globe, probably deciding whether to spin it again. After a few seconds he shrugged and walked out, the cigar still clenched in his teeth. I followed him to the hall, but he was out the front door before I could open it for him.

"Well?" I said to Wolfe back in the office.

"Mr. Cramer wants very badly to believe he has the murderer," he said, "but he's troubled. And he's far too honest to take the easy way out by sacrificing an innocent person, merely to avoid pressure from his superiors."

"The notes," I said.

"Of course." Wolfe nodded. "They complicate the situation, and Mr. Cramer obviously realizes this. Why would the murderer, be it Mr. Milner or someone else, alert his intended victim with a warning?"

"Maybe they were sent by someone else," I ventured. "A coincidence. Stevens apparently had plenty of detractors."

"Pah!" Wolfe waved my suggestion aside. "Without question the same person who wrote the notes also is the murderer. Could you conceive of doing such a thing yourself, if you were planning to destroy someone?"

"Nope," I said. "Too much effort, and as you said, all it does is make the target more careful."

"Your reaction is normal," Wolfe said, laying a hand palm down on his blotter, "and it would be mine as well. But whoever killed Milan Stevens detested him so intensely that the notes were used as additional means of inflicting discomfort. And the murderer was so confident of ultimate success that he—or she—felt this extra measure of sadistic satisfaction outweighed any dangers." He glanced at the clock on the wall. "Try again to get Miss Radovich."

I turned to dial the number while Wolfe picked up his receiver. This time I got rings instead of a busy signal, and a female voice I didn't recognize answered.

"I'm sorry, but Miss Radovich is resting right now and can't be disturbed," she said.

"Can you please tell her it's Mr. Goodwin?"

"Really, she isn't—"

"Please, at least tell her and let her decide for herself."

The woman left the phone. After about a minute, Maria was on the line. "I know you've been through hell in the last twelve hours," I said, "but Mr. Wolfe is anxious to see you. Can you come this afternoon?"

"Yes—I was going to call you. I took sleeping pills, and just now got up. I want badly to see you and talk about Jerry. What time should I come?" she asked in a fuzzy voice.

"Three?" I asked. It was as much a question to Wolfe as to Maria. He nodded, and she said she'd be there. I hung up and turned to say something to him, but his nose was in a book, where it would stay until Fritz announced lunch.

8

After finishing lunch, I walked over to Eighth Avenue and picked up the afternoon papers. Both the *Gazette* and the *Post* played the murder as the banner, and each had a big picture of Stevens on the front page. The *Gazette* story jumped inside to a page that also had articles on Stevens's career and violence in New York today. There was a mention of Wolfe's role and pictures of both of us. Most of what I'd fed to Lon was in the main story, along with a diagram of the library, showing the position of Stevens's body when we found it. Maria wasn't quoted anywhere, though—the story said she was "in seclusion."

No mention was made of Gerald Milner in either paper, but each said the police commissioner and the district attorney had scheduled a joint press conference for three o'clock "to announce a major development in the case." In the meantime, citizens' groups were making noise, and the head of one had asked in print: "What kind of city is this that not even one of its most prominent and highly respected residents is safe in his own home?" The mayor called the murder "a terrible, senseless tragedy," but said he had complete confidence that the police would move with dispatch to find the murderer.

Wolfe was at his desk reading when I got back. "It's all over the papers now," I said, laying them in front of him. "By the way, I think we need to give out new pictures to the press. Yours doesn't do justice to your graying temples. Mine on the other hand makes me look older than I really—"

"Archie, shut up!"

"Yes, sir. Anyway, the commissioner and the D.A. have called a press conference for three—the same time Maria will be here. It's sure to be on Milner, after what Cramer told us. Shall I get Lon and ask him to call us when his reporter phones in with the story?"

Wolfe nodded as he opened the papers and began reading. Like almost everyone else, he likes to see his name in print, and he turned quickly to the page with our pictures. He read for a minute, then looked up. "Assuming Mr. Milner is to be charged with murder, will a bail be set?"

"Probably," I answered, "although it's likely to be a big one."

I had expected Maria to be early, so when the doorbell rang at seven minutes to three, I wasn't surprised. Through the one-way glass, I could see she was alone and wearing sunglasses, despite the overcast day. I opened the door, gave her a sympathetic smile, and helped her off with her coat.

I won't say Wolfe never rises for a woman, but it doesn't happen often. That day, though, he was on his feet when Maria entered the office and remained standing until I had parked her in the red leather chair.

"You have our most sincere sympathies," he said. "I can't speak to your uncle's musical prowess, as I have no frame of reference, but I can say that he was a man of dedication, character, and great bravery, and I do not use those words carelessly."

"Thank you," Maria said hoarsely. She kept her sunglasses on.

"It goes without saying," he continued, "that we all, you, me, Mr. Goodwin, want the same thing—the arrest and conviction of your uncle's killer, whoever that may be. Before we go on, however, one point: Inspector Cramer of Homicide was here earlier, and he suggested that Mr. Goodwin and I were at least indirectly responsible for your uncle's death because we did not immediately turn those notes over to the police. Do you agree?"

"No—not at all," Maria said, leaning forward in the chair. "Even if we had gone against his wishes and taken the notes to the police, Uncle Milos wouldn't have cooperated. He would have said the whole thing was nonsense."

"I gathered as much from what you said on your earlier visit," Wolfe said, "but I wanted to establish your confidence in both of us."

"Absolutely," Maria said. "When I first came here, I wanted to find out who was writing the notes. This time, I want you to find a murderer, and I suppose now . . . I'll be able to afford whatever fee you ask." She looked down at her hands in her lap and shrugged. "But I know it can't be Jerry. I'm positive. He's just not . . ." The words trailed off.

"Madam," Wolfe said, "first, do not concern yourself about payment. As I said on your earlier visit, I have a debt of considerable magnitude to your late uncle. Second, when I undertake an investigation, there can be no constraints, no limitations. It may be that Mr. Milner is guilty. If so—"

"No!" Maria said. "Violence is not in his nature."

"Throughout history, passion has driven otherwise

gentle individuals to extreme acts of violence," Wolfe remarked dryly. "I'm merely trying to establish that however unpleasant the truth may be to you, all pertinent information must eventually reach the police. But because we're now on the subject of Mr. Milner and because the police consider him a prime suspect, I have questions."

Maria nodded.

"When you first sat in that chair, it was obvious that your concern over the notes centered at least partially on who had written them. Did you fear Mr. Milner was their author?"

"Mr. Wolfe, I was worried about my uncle." Maria took off the sunglasses and shifted in the big chair. She looked like she hadn't slept in days.

"And with good reason, as it turned out," Wolfe said. "Madam, we must be candid with each other. I know that your uncle and Mr. Milner had argued. Am I correct that you were the cause?"

"Yes. I met Jerry several months ago while I was waiting for my uncle at Symphony Hall. We started seeing each other after that, and . . ." She gestured as if to explain.

"Was your uncle aware of this friendship?" Wolfe asked.

"No. Uncle Milos never approved of anybody I went out with. And he told me once that musicians made terrible husbands. For a long time—several months—we met secretly. But"—again Maria gestured—"we fell in love, and Jerry said he wanted to marry me."

"Your response?" Wolfe asked.

"I told him I wanted to marry him, too, but I was afraid of what my uncle would say. Jerry said he would talk to him about it, but I told him I was sure Uncle Milos would be furious and that it might hurt Jerry's career with the orchestra."

"But he spoke to your uncle anyway?"

"Yes, about three weeks ago, and it was just as I had expected. I wasn't there, but Jerry told me later that after a rehearsal, he followed my uncle back to his dressing room, and on the way he told him about us. Uncle Milos became terribly angry, and he shouted at Jerry, right there in the hallway backstage, where a lot of other people heard it."

"When did you first learn about the incident?" Wolfe asked.

"Jerry called me right after it happened. He said Uncle Milos threatened to dismiss him from the Symphony, and told him that they could easily do without him. Jerry was very upset when he called me. He said he was willing to leave the orchestra if it came to that, but he was still determined we should marry, whether or not my uncle gave his blessing. I told him he shouldn't do anything to endanger his career, that I would talk to my uncle and see if I could reason with him.

"Uncle Milos came home a little while later, but before I could even begin, he said, 'I don't want you to see that Milner again; how could you be interested in such a man? He is beneath you, and he's only an adequate musician, as well!' He told me he believed the only reason Jerry was interested in me was that he thought it would improve his position in the orchestra. I said I thought the very opposite was true, that Jerry knew his feelings about me might very well damage him. But Uncle Milos wouldn't discuss it anymore."

"Did you pursue the subject later?" Wolfe asked.

"I tried several times in the next few days, but always he refused to talk about Jerry at all. He would walk out of the room when I tried to bring it up."

The telephone rang, and I turned to answer. It was Lon.

"Archie, our guy called from Centre Street a couple minutes ago, and it was like we figured. They've charged Milner with murder. The commissioner and the D.A.

spent most of the press conference congratulating each other on the fast work, et cetera. They set bond at a quarter-million. I gotta run."

"Thank you very much," I said in a businesslike voice, hanging up and turning back to Wolfe. "That was Mr. Wilson. He called to confirm the details of our earlier discussion and to say the price is two-five-oh."

Wolfe nodded and addressed Maria. "Madam, I will repeat the question I asked earlier and which you side-stepped: When you first talked to us about the notes, did you not fear that they had been written by Mr. Milner?"

She took a deep breath. "I . . . suppose so. Jerry was so depressed about what had happened that I was afraid he might have done something foolish, just to scare my uncle. But he could never have killed anyone. He—"

"Yes, I know," Wolfe said. "You need not further stress your feelings about Mr. Milner. Did you ever mention the notes to him?"

"No," Maria said. "I saw no reason to . . . upset him further."

"I will repeat another question I asked on your earlier visit: Was there anyone in the Symphony who might have wanted your uncle dead?"

"I can't think of anyone. I said before, there are tensions and jealousies, but they always seem to exist in great orchestras. But any murderous hatred—no, not that I was aware of."

Wolfe pursed his lips. "Miss Radovich, were you and your uncle satisfied with your apartment building?"

"He was never very interested in where we lived," Maria said. "When we first came to New York, we stayed for several months in a hotel on Central Park South that is popular with music people. It wasn't a bad place, but Uncle Milos wanted something larger, so we found this building. He bought the apartment right away after we'd seen it. I didn't think it was as nice as we should have had—on his earnings, he could have afforded much better. But it satisfied him. Mr. Remmers tried to convince him to move into a bigger, more expensive building. He said the conductor of the New York Symphony merited something better, but my uncle is—was—very stubborn. And he was very much taken with the library in this apartment. He said it was a nice place to work. And then that's where . . ." Maria stopped and looked down, resting her head on one hand.

"Did you find the security adequate?" Wolfe asked.

Maria nodded. "I suppose so, although again, Mr. Remmers said we should be in a building with better protection. But there was always a hallman on duty, and in the daytime, a doorman too."

"Is someone in your apartment during the day?"

"We have a maid who comes Mondays through Fridays, from about ten in the morning until three," Maria said.

"Do you have a cook as well?" Wolfe asked.

"No, we usually eat out, although sometimes I make something for the two of us."

Wolfe grimaced. The thought of anyone not having a cook always disturbs him. "I have another appointment," he said, glancing at the wall clock, "but before we conclude, you should know that Mr. Milner has been charged with murder."

Maria stiffened, but otherwise showed little emotion; the last two days had probably sucked most of the emotion out of her, and she looked to be on the ragged edge. "I must see him—I haven't talked to him since . . . since before it happened." She turned to me and back to Wolfe again.

"I plan to post bond for Mr. Milner," Wolfe said. "You will be able to see him then. However, it is also imperative that I see him—here. Will I need your help to convince him to come?"

"Jerry will do anything I ask of him," Maria said.

"Good," Wolfe said. "One more question before you leave: Would you have married Mr. Milner against your uncle's wishes?"

Maria looked steadily at Wolfe. "I was prepared for once to defy Uncle Milos," she said.

"Very well. Mr. Goodwin and I will keep you apprised of developments." For the second time that afternoon, Wolfe rose in a woman's presence.

"I'll get you a cab," I said as I helped her on with her coat in the hall. "Is anyone staying with you?"

Maria said no. "Some friends have asked me to move in with them for a few days, but . . . I haven't really wanted to be around anybody."

"You shouldn't be in that place alone. I know a woman with a large apartment, and she'd be glad to have you stay with her for a while. She's in and out a lot, and you'd have plenty of privacy."

Maria balked, but I persuaded her that she'd be happier away from the murder scene. "I'll stop back there with you later, and you can pick up some clothes," I said as I put her in a cab and gave her Lily Rowan's name and address. When I got back inside, Wolfe was standing in the hall.

"Call Mr. Parker," he said. "Tell him to get Mr. Milner out of jail as soon as possible. I want him here tonight, after dinner. Draw the necessary amount from the bank for bail." Having fulfilled his role as resident order-giver, he rode the elevator up for his two-hour afternoon commune with the orchids, leaving me with the mundane responsibility of carrying out those orders.

9

I don't think Nero Wolfe has ever properly appreciated my role as the fulfiller of his wishes. During the one hundred and twenty minutes he was puttering with his playthings up on the roof that afternoon, I was making hurried telephone calls, jumping into and out of taxis, and signing a cashier's check for twenty-five thousand dollars. All so that when he rode the elevator down and walked into his office, I could turn in my chair and casually say, "Everything's set; Milner's out and will be here at nine."

It's not that my efforts were totally overlooked. After all, he did say "Very satisfactory" when he sat down, which is roughly equivalent to a lesser mortal clicking his heels, doing a cartwheel, and singing the first two verses of "Yankee Doodle Dandy."

I've got to brag a little about those two hours, although I did get a few breaks. The instant the elevator doors closed behind Wolfe, I was on the phone to Lily, who was home. Break Number One. She was only mildly miffed at me for sending an unannounced houseguest her way, one who was en route to her Park Avenue palace even as we talked. Her interest increased when she learned it was the niece of the late Milan Stevens.

"Escamillo, am I to assume this has something to do with your preoccupation of the other evening?"

"You may assume whatever you wish, my love. I can't give you any details right now, but I promise I will somewhere along the way. In the meantime, please make Maria feel at home, as only you can do. I don't have to tell you the state she's in, and that rest and privacy are what she needs more than anything. By the way, she'll be coming without a suitcase."

"I'm sure I can find things to fit her," Lily said. "Worry no more, she'll find a safe haven here. When will I hear from you again? And do I have any other instructions?"

I told Lily I'd call her again that day, and maybe even see her, then I dialed the number of Nathaniel Parker, who for years has been Wolfe's lawyer and the only member of the bar that he trusts. He was in his office— Break Number Two.

"Archie! I haven't heard from you in months. Is everything well with you and Wolfe?"

"More or less," I told him. "I'm calling on business, of all things. Mr. Wolfe wants to post the bond for Gerald Milner, the man who's been charged with Milan Stevens's murder."

"What! I just heard about that on the radio a little while ago. I . . . There are a dozen questions I'd like to ask. First, what's the bond?"

"A quarter-million," I said.

Parker made a sound somewhere between a whistle and a wheeze. "That means, depending on the judge, it'll probably take twenty-five grand to get him out."

"No problem," I said. "Look, our bank closes in less

than an hour, and we want Milner free right away. Can you meet me at the Thirty-fourth Street branch of the Metropolitan Trust Company in fifteen minutes?"

Parker sounded a little dazed, but said he'd cancel an appointment and be there. I told Fritz to cover the phone, and I was out the door in search of a cab, which I quickly found. Break Number Three. Traffic was unusually light for that time of day, so I got to the bank in ten minutes. I waited in front, and shortly another taxi pulled up: Nathaniel Parker, attorney-at-law, unfolded his six feet, four inches and stepped out. "Good to see you, Archie, despite the ... *unusual* circumstances," he said, holding out a big hand. "I just called the court, and as I suspected, it's a ten-percent bail, so you've got to cough up twenty-five thousand."

After that, things moved pretty fast. I went inside and talked to Mr. Tucker, the branch manager, with whom Wolfe and I had been dealing for years. Ten minutes later, Parker had a cashier's check in his pocket and was in a cab on his way to get Gerald Milner out of the Riker's Island Detention Center, while I was in a taxi of my own heading for Lily Rowan's apartment.

Lily was surprised to see me so soon, and said Maria had checked in and was lying down. "You're about to have another visitor, although not as a houseguest," I told her, looking at my watch. "If all goes well, the man charged with Milan Stevens's murder will be walking through that door in the next half-hour."

It's hard to shock Lily Rowan, but that time I managed. Her mouth dropped open, and her first words were, "I need a drink." I said I'd have one myself, and after I mixed two Scotch-and-waters, we sat in Lily's sunroom while I sketched in the situation, figuring I owed it to her. Lily's not one to be fazed by anything for long, and I could see her eyes sparkle as she realized she was being drawn into the case. We had agreed on her role for the evening when the call came from downstairs: Mr. Nathaniel Parker and another gentleman were here to see Miss Rowan.

Lily was nervous as we waited for the elevator to bring them up. I'll admit I was a little on edge myself, and particularly curious to see what kind of guy Gerald Milner was. I can hardly say he made a good first impression, but maybe part of the problem is that when two men enter a room together and one is eight inches taller than the other, the little guy is starting with a couple of strikes. After getting used to his height—he barely reached Parker's shoulders—I began sizing Milner up: horn-rimmed glasses, sandy hair that fell over one eye, slightly stooped shoulders, and a glum expression, which was certainly understandable under the circumstances. He was wearing a blue suit and a white dress shirt open at the collar. And he looked totally lost.

"Mr. Milner, this is Miss Lily Rowan and Mr. Archie Goodwin," Parker said formally. I was expecting a limp paw, but I got a surprisingly strong handshake. That's one in your favor, I thought, but I still wonder what Maria sees in you.

"Mr. Milner, Mr. Parker, please come in and sit down," Lily said, gesturing toward her ballroom-sized living room. "I'm sure you'd both like a drink; Mr. Goodwin is taking orders." She smiled sweetly at me, and I made for the bar. Parker took his usual dry martini, and Milner, who must have wondered what the hell was going on, asked for a sherry. I refilled Lily's and my Scotch, and we all sat looking at each other.

"Any problems?" I asked Parker. "Anybody from the press there when you posted bond?"

"Not a soul," Parker said. "It went very smoothly. Although"—he turned to Milner—"I think this gentleman was most surprised at finding himself free."

"Yes," Milner said in a strong voice that didn't go with the rest of him. "I'm wondering who I have to thank, and why. I'm happy, of course, but—"

He stopped talking and stared over my left shoulder. I turned and saw Maria standing in the doorway wearing a robe. They looked at each other without saying anything, and finally Maria, unconscious of how she was dressed, ran over and embraced him as he stood up. "I've been so worried," she said, burying her face in his chest.

"It's all right," he said. "As long as you know it wasn't me, everything's all right."

Lily stood and eyed Parker and me. "Gentlemen, I suggest we finish our drinks in the sunroom and let these two have a few minutes together."

We dutifully filed out, but Maria and Milner hardly noticed. At that point, they would have been oblivious of anything that measured less than seven on the Richter scale. "I know you both have a lot of questions about what's going on," I said as we took our seats in the sunroom. "I've got to get back home now and report to you-know-who, but eventually I'll explain all of it. You're having the two lovers for dinner, right?" I asked Lily, and she nodded. "Okay, Mr. Wolfe wants to see Milner at nine. The three of you can come over in a cab, because I doubt that the two of them will want to be apart for long, and you can keep Maria company in the front room while we're talking. I don't think Milner will balk at coming, especially after Maria explains to him that we're the ones who sprung him."

I turned to Parker: "You said everything went smoothly getting Milner out. Does that also mean Mr. Wolfe's name wasn't connected with the bond in any way?"

"Right, Archie, although everybody in town knows I'm Nero Wolfe's attorney, so it won't take a great intellect to figure out who was behind the move."

"True enough," I said, "but at least they'll harass you first, before coming to us." Parker smiled and allowed as how he could handle the harassment just fine. At that, we both stood, thanking Lily for the hospitality.

"Think nothing of it," she said in a low voice. "I have last-second overnight guests and suspected murderers as dinner companions all the time."

I scratched my right cheek just below the ear and winked at her as we walked out. Parker and I went our separate ways in taxis, with mine delivering me to the brownstone at a quarter to six. I had time to clean up a little of the deskwork before Wolfe came down and I gave him the word that everything was ready.

After his "Very satisfactory" and a ring for beer, he asked for a verbatim fill-in. He was particularly interested in my reaction to Milner. "Short, meek, generally unimpressive to look at, but he has a strong handshake," I said. "As I told you, I didn't hear him speak more than a sentence or two, but there's something about him I like. Your next question is: Do I think he killed Stevens? My gut reaction is nine-to-two against, but don't ask me to explain it, because I can't—except that I don't think he's capable of killing anything larger than a full-grown mosquito."

Wolfe poured the first bottle of beer into his glass and drained half of it. "Assuming that I form a similar opinion after talking to Mr. Milner, I suggest we have him stay here, at least tonight. Do you think it absolutely necessary for Miss Radovich and Miss Rowan to accompany him here?"

I said yes, it was a good idea to have them come along. Maria would ensure that Milner came, and Lily in turn was insurance that the twosome wouldn't have an irrational last-minute impulse to fly off to God-knows-where. Wolfe shrugged, resigning himself to having two women under his roof for a few hours. The very thought was enough to make him ring for more beer.

10

I'd like to be able to report that Wolfe's session with Gerald Milner was productive and stimulating, but that would be overstating things. Actually, the evening started well enough, with the three of them—Maria, Lily, and Milner—arriving right at nine, after Wolfe and I had finished off Fritz's veal birds à l'italienne and two helpings of pecan pie, with ample time left over for coffee in the office.

I answered the bell, and after relieving them of their coats in the hall, ushered all three into the office. This time Wolfe stayed glued to his chair as I introduced Milner and said something about how Lily hadn't been over in some time.

Wolfe tilted his head at the women. "I'd invite you to sit, but I think Mr. Goodwin has explained the need for us to talk alone to Mr. Milner. You're welcome to stay in the front room, and Mr. Brenner can serve you dessert and coffee or some other beverage if you wish."

"I've already spoken to Maria about this," Lily said

with a smile, "and what she'd really like is to look at your orchids. For that matter, I never get tired of seeing them myself."

"Indeed?" Wolfe said. Lily knew that one guaranteed route to Wolfe's vanity was to ask to see the orchids—it was a request he almost never denied. Theodore was visiting his sister in New Jersey, so Wolfe buzzed Fritz, who instantly materialized in the doorway. "Fritz, would you please accompany Miss Rowan and Miss Radovich to the plant rooms? They can stay as long as they wish, and afterward they may want dessert or other refreshment in the front room." Fritz ushered the women out, and I aimed Milner at the red leather chair, settling in at my desk with notebook and pen.

Wolfe eyed our guest. "Mr. Milner, would you like anything to drink? Coffee, perhaps? A cocktail?"

"No, nothing, thank you," Milner said. He seemed just as ill-at-ease as when he'd walked into Lily's apartment a few hours earlier. "There are some questions I'd like to ask, though," he said, clearing his throat.

"No doubt," Wolfe replied. "And likely you'll get answers in the course of our discussion. Please indulge me first, however. As you've probably been told, I posted your bond." Milner nodded. "You also probably know I am acting on behalf of Miss Radovich." Another nod.

Wolfe shifted in the chair. "I've been hired by Miss Radovich to find the murderer of her uncle. She is convinced of your innocence, although I begin with no such preconception. Any investigation of Milan Stevens's death must begin with you, and because I never leave this house on business, it was necessary for you to come here."

"Yes, but—"

"If you please, Mr. Milner," Wolfe said, turning over a hand. "Let me continue. The most expeditious way to get through the evening is by humoring me. First—did you kill Milan Stevens?"

Milner sighed and looked up. "I can't begin to tell you how many times I've been asked that by the police," he said in a tired voice. "Sometimes they phrased it as a question, other times they made it sound like an outright statement and dared me to contradict them. But my answer was always the same: No, I didn't kill him. I couldn't have; I probably respected him more than just about any man I've ever known."

"I realize I'm trailing the herd, Mr. Milner, and I must of necessity trample some of the same grass it did. Your forbearance, please, if the questions are ones you've heard before." Wolfe shifted again and reached for the buzzer to ring for beer before remembering that Fritz wasn't in the kitchen. He scowled and went on. "It has been established that you were in the Stevens apartment the night of the murder. Why?"

Another sigh. "I suppose it doesn't matter how often I tell it," Milner said, "it still sounds strange. But here's what happened: On Wednesday—my God, that's just` yesterday—a note in a sealed envelope was left for me in the musicians' lounge at Symphony Hall after rehearsal. It was from Mr. Stevens, asking me to come to his apartment that night at eight-fifteen. The note said it was very important that I be there."

"How did you know it was from Mr. Stevens?" Wolfe asked.

"The note was on his paper—one of those small sheets with 'From the desk of Milan Stevens' printed at the top."

"Was it handwritten?"

"No, typed," Milner said, running a hand through his already ruffled hair.

"I suppose the police have the note?"

"Nobody has it," Milner said glumly. "I threw it away, I think right there in the lounge wastebasket."

"Do you recall the wording?" Wolfe asked. "Be as precise as you can."

Milner hunched his shoulders. "It was a short note—only a few sentences. It started with my name at the top, and then said something like 'Please be at my apartment tonight at eight-fifteen. I have a matter of extreme importance to discuss with you.' I think that was all."

"Was the note signed?"

"No, his name was typed at the bottom. There was no writing on the sheet at all—I'm sure of that," Milner said.

"Was Mr. Stevens in the habit of communicating with you this way?" Wolfe asked.

"No, that was the first note I ever got from him."

"Didn't you think it strange to receive such a message from your conductor?"

"Maybe a little," Milner conceded, "but under the circumstances, there were . . . at least two reasons why he might have wanted to see me."

"Go on," Wolfe commanded.

"I haven't seen much of Maria the last few days, so I don't know whether she told you about . . ." He trailed off and looked glumly at Wolfe.

"About your asking Milan Stevens's blessing to marry his niece?" Wolfe asked, finishing his sentence.

Milner nodded. "I thought he either wanted to talk to me about that or . . ." Again he halted, but this time he managed to find his tongue: ". . . maybe he was going to ask me to resign from the orchestra."

"Indeed? Because you had asked for his niece's hand, or because of your performance as a musician?"

Milner colored slightly. "I suppose you'd have to ask others about my ability, but I feel I've been doing well. I'm one of the newer members, though; this is only my second season with the Symphony."

"And before that?"

"I was with the Indianapolis Symphony for four years;

previously, I had taught music for two years, right after getting a graduate degree."

"Mr. Milner, did you tell anyone you were going to Stevens's apartment?"

"No, nobody. I live alone, and my family are all in the Midwest. I have no really close friends, so there would have been no one to tell except Maria, and I thought it best not to say anything at all to her about it."

"I'd like to go back," Wolfe said, "to the day you told Stevens you wanted to marry Miss Radovich. Can you recall precisely when that was?"

"The police asked the same question, and I had to think about it for a while; it was the day we were rehearsing Tchaikovsky's Fourth Symphony, which would have been three weeks ago yesterday."

"As I understand it, his reaction was violent."

"That's putting it mildly, Mr. Wolfe," Milner said, combing his hair with his fingers again. "I stopped him in the corridor that leads back to his dressing room, which was a mistake. He was in a hurry to begin with, and became irritated when I asked if I could speak to him. But that was nothing compared to what followed." Milner shifted in his chair and looked at Wolfe, who nodded his head an eighth of an inch.

"I blurted out right there in the hallway that Maria and I wanted to get married. He started shouting and telling me that under no circumstances would he allow his niece to become the wife of a musician, let alone one of what he called 'my caliber.' People who were walking by turned to stare at us. It was terrible."

"Had Mr. Stevens criticized your work before?" Wolfe asked.

"No more than other members'. You must remember that he was very hard to please, and frequently became impatient with individuals or whole sections of the orchestra. But he had never indicated to me in any way that I wasn't competent."

"Did you respond to him after his tirade?"

"No, I was so taken aback I couldn't think of anything to say. Besides, after he got done, he turned away and went straight to his dressing room. I just stood there feeling foolish and watching him."

"How did he behave toward you after that?"

Milner bit his lip. "A few times in rehearsals lately—since that day in the hall—he's made sarcastic comments about me, even though they weren't called for. Things like 'If we can have Mr. Milner's attention, maybe we can continue now.' Even though I was paying attention all the time. Others noticed it too. One of the other players stopped me in the hall after a rehearsal and asked, 'What's up? Why's the Old Man got it in for you?' The situation was getting very uncomfortable."

"Had you ever encountered Mr. Stevens when you picked Miss Radovich up at their apartment?" Wolfe asked.

"Oh, no!" Milner said in a tone that suggested Wolfe had no understanding of the situation. "Until that day in the hall, he didn't know we were seeing each other—Maria wanted it that way. I only went to the apartment to get her when he wasn't there. Otherwise, we would just meet somewhere."

"Knowing something about Stevens's personality and his proprietary feeling about his niece, should you have been surprised at his reaction?" Wolfe asked.

Milner shrugged. "I suppose not; it was a stupid thing to do. I should have listened to Maria and let her break it to him, but I felt it was my responsibility."

"Pride of the male," Wolfe said. "Let us get to the fateful night. Am I correct that you didn't call the Stevens apartment before going there?"

"No—that is, yes, I didn't call. I stayed in Manhattan all day after rehearsals, rather than going home—I live out in Queens. Maria had rehearsals of her own, so we didn't see each other, which was just as well. I was terribly nervous about that night, and I hardly had anything to eat for lunch or dinner."

"I repeat an earlier question: Did you tell anyone where you were going?"

"No, nobody. The police asked me what I did all day, and I guess you want to know too. I stopped in several bookstores to browse. That usually takes my mind off my troubles, but it didn't help, so I went up to Central Park and walked a lot and sat on benches. I tried to do some thinking, mostly about Maria and what I'd do if I lost my job with the orchestra. It was cold, but I hardly noticed it. I must have been in the park three hours or more."

"And then?"

"More walking, and finally I stopped in a coffee shop on Lexington, where I mainly sat and stared at my dinner. By then, it was past eight, and I had to take a cab to get to the apartment on time."

Wolfe looked at Milner, but said nothing. He still wanted beer, but he wasn't going to ask me to get it for him, and I wasn't about to offer.

The silence and the gaze made Milner uneasy, so he went on: "I got to the apartment and asked for Mr. Stevens in the lobby. Now, this is what I don't understand: The hallman called upstairs and said I was there, and Mr. Stevens told him to send me up. But two or three minutes later, when I got there . . ."

"Go on," Wolfe said.

"I think you pretty much know the rest. When I got off the elevator, the apartment door was standing open. I said 'Anyone home?' twice, or maybe three times, and then I knocked loudly. No answer, so I walked in and called Mr. Stevens's name again. And Maria's too, on the chance that she might be home. There was a light on in the living room, but nobody there. Then I walked into the library and saw him lying in the corner."

"And you fled the apartment at that point?"

"No, I went over to him, and when I got there, I saw the blood, and the knife on the floor—I guess it was really a letter opener. I knelt next to him, feeling for a pulse. There wasn't any, though, and I was sure he was dead."

"Mr. Milner, I'm confident you would describe yourself as a responsible citizen, reared with a respect for the law," Wolfe said. "Why didn't you call the police?"

"As I told Inspector Cramer, I panicked. I guess I was thinking about how bad it would have looked for me, although I can't reconstruct what was going on in my mind at the time—and I've tried. All I remember is leaving the apartment, taking the elevator down, and walking out the front door."

"Other than the hallman, did you encounter anyone in the building?"

"Nobody. I was alone in the elevator going up and coming down, and there was no one else in the lobby or the upstairs entrance hall."

"Where did you go after you left the building?"

"I just walked again, this time up and down Fifth and Madison and Park and Lexington, all over Manhattan until past midnight. I tried to sort things out. I knew I was in big trouble—I'd given the hallman my name and all, but I couldn't face up to going to the police, and I certainly couldn't call Maria. I finally took the subway to Queens, and on the way I decided to call the police when I got home. But as you know, they were already there, waiting outside for me." Milner took a deep breath and slumped in the chair, looking like he'd just completed the Boston Marathon.

Wolfe didn't look so hot himself. For the last several minutes, he'd been in a pout, and rather than risk having him quit in the middle of the evening, I decided to play the man of action. "Look," I said, "you two have been at it for well over an hour, and I think drinks are in order. Mr. Milner?"

"Yes, yes, I will have something now, thanks. Do you have sherry?" I told him we did, both dry and sweet, and he said he'd take dry. I went to the liquor cabinet and poured him a glass, which I placed on the small table at his elbow. Then, without a word, I left the office and went down the hall to the kitchen, where I got two cold bottles of beer from the refrigerator and a tall glass from the shelf. I put all three on a tray and went back, trying to imitate Fritz's walk as I entered the room. I placed the tray in front of Wolfe with what I thought was a suitable flourish. He glowered at me, and his "Thank you" had icicles all over it. I shrugged and went back to the liquor cabinet, where I poured myself two fingers of bourbon before getting settled again.

After he'd drained about a half-glass and dabbed his lips with his handkerchief, Wolfe considered Milner again. "You have proclaimed your innocence; would you care to speculate on Mr. Stevens's killer?"

Milner set his glass down and stared at it. "I really can't," he said. "I've thought about it a lot the last couple of days, as you might guess. But I simply don't know who would have wanted to kill him."

"What about other members of the orchestra? Were there any who might bear him a special grudge?"

"A special grudge? I don't know," Milner said between sips of sherry. "Musicians often resent their conductor, particularly if he pushes them hard, as Mr. Stevens did. I never heard more than what I think of as the usual amount of grumbling, though. Except . . ."

"Yes?" Wolfe prompted.

"Well, a while back, there was a lot of talk around the lounge backstage that Mr. Hirsch, the associate conductor, had wanted the job as music director when Mr. Stevens was named. But that all happened a few months before I joined the orchestra. If there's any bad feeling between them, I haven't been aware of it."

For another hour-plus, Wolfe pumped Milner on the orchestra and its people, but he didn't get enough out of him to fill a small bucket. It was evident that Milner was right about himself in at least one respect: He was far down the totem pole at the Symphony, and had little knowledge of its movers and shakers.

"Mr. Milner, it's getting late," Wolfe said, "and we've covered those areas that interest me. Have all of your own questions been answered?"

He managed a weak smile. "Yes, I think so, although I still wonder who wrote those notes to Mr. Stevens. The police of course insist it was me."

"That's what they want to believe," Wolfe said. "And since the notes were neither typed nor handwritten, but printed, proof of authorship is difficult. Now, if you'll excuse Mr. Goodwin and me, we need to talk for a few minutes. Archie, show Mr. Milner to the front room. The others must be down by now."

I refilled Milner's sherry glass and steered him across the hall, where Lily and Maria were drinking coffee. Maria popped up when she saw her man, and started right in asking him questions before I cut in. "Pardon me, but Mr. Wolfe and I need to confer. Has Fritz been good to you?"

Lily spoke. "We just came down from the plant rooms, and I think Maria was as impressed as I always am. And yes, Fritz has been a dear." Maria gave me an obligatory smile and then shifted her attention back to Milner. No accounting for taste, I thought, closing the door behind me.

"Well?" Wolfe demanded as I lit in my chair.

"Well, what?" I shot back. "Well, am I tired? Hell, yes. Well, has Milner been a help to us? Not much. Well, do I think I can steal Maria away from him? Maybe, given a little time. Well, are we—"

"Confound it, stop blathering. You know very well what I'm asking."

I shrugged and turned my palms up. "I'll hold my odds at nine-to-two against, unless he's a far better actor than he seems. I think the guy would find it tough to stomp on an ant, let alone carve up a maestro. But the law's feeling a lot of pressure on this one."

Wolfe nodded. "That pressure is undoubtedly intense, and Mr. Milner provides a convenient solution, which is precisely what the murderer planned on."

"Yeah, it looks that way. But who? And how did the killer get into the apartment?"

Wolfe ignored the questions. "Call Miss Radovich in. She's entitled to know our position, and that we're prepared to go on."

I got Maria from across the hall, and Wolfe gave her the good news—at least it was good compared to most of what she'd been getting lately. She was so happy about someone else believing in Milner's innocence that I thought she was going to start the waterworks right there, which would have sent Wolfe running to his room. But she got herself under control and tried again to bring up the subject of fees. Wolfe deflected it and said the best thing she could give us was total cooperation all along the way. His first request was that she persuade Milner to stay with us, at least for the night. "Bond has been posted," he said, "and neither the police nor the district attorney's office should have any need for him for at least a few days. If he remains here, he'll be away from the press and their probings, and he'll also be readily available should we have any further questions about the workings of the orchestra."

I thought he was laying it on a little heavy, but it sold Maria. When he was finished, she said she'd go right in and talk to him about bunking with us.

"You really think it's necessary to keep him here?" I asked after she had left the room and closed the door behind her. The last person to stay in the South Room had been blown apart by a bomb concealed in an aluminum cigar tube, but I could see no reason to mention that now.

"Why not?" Wolfe answered with a shrug. "It gives us better control of the situation. And indeed, as we go on we may have need of Mr. Milner's opinions concerning his fellow musicians. Miss Radovich will be back quickly, telling us that he has agreed to stay. After you escort the women to the door and get Fritz to take Mr. Milner to the South Room, I have some instructions."

He was showing off, although in this case it hardly required a crystal-ball gazer to predict the result. Maria took about forty-five seconds to talk Milner into staying with us—I found out later from Lily that she handled it like a major general giving orders to a corporal. And it was no problem having Fritz get our new guest settled in the South Room, which is two flights up, on the same floor as my bedroom and directly above Wolfe's. But I wasn't about to abandon two lovely women at our front door, so the three of us walked all the way to Eighth Avenue before I reeled in a cab and sent them off with fond farewells.

This meant it was at least twenty minutes before I got back to the office, where Wolfe had found refuge in a book. He glared as I slipped into my chair, and then proceeded to outline the next day's plans. They were skimpier than I had hoped, but compared to the last two years, they were downright invigorating. In fact, as I took notes, I almost began to feel like a working man again.

11

Friday was among the more memorable days in the recent history of the old brownstone, for a variety of reasons. It started out in a frustrating way, which I attribute to the rustiness of idle machinery, and Wolfe and I had been idle for a long time.

To start with, I slept longer than I should have, but I was still catching up on what I'd lost two nights ago. At eight-forty-five I hit the kitchen after having stopped in the South Room, where our guest was not only in one piece, but was working on a breakfast tray nearly as well filled as Wolfe's. I told him to stay in his room until further notice, as we might be having visitors, and he nodded between bites of a blueberry muffin.

The phone rang when I was barely halfway through my first cup of coffee and still on page one of the *Times*. Fritz answered on the kitchen extension and cupped the receiver: "For you, Archie. Mr. Cohen."

I said a word that made Fritz blush and told him I'd take it in the office. The top item on my instructions from Wolfe had been to call Lon. "You're not going to believe this," I said into the phone at my desk, "but right here in my notebook is a numeral 'one' and after it a notation to call Lon Cohen first thing Friday morning."

"You're right, I don't believe it," came the reply. "Archie, how long have we known each other? Don't I rate a few breaks from you?" I started to say something, but Lon went right on. "One of our beat guys— admittedly a few hours late—discovered this morning that Milner's out on bond and that the bail was posted by your old friend Nathaniel Parker. More than coincidence, I'd say. Milner's not at his apartment in Queens. And we've already tried to reach Parker, too, but there's no answer at his office and his wife says he's already left home for work. So, on the off-chance you might know something about this, I decided to—"

"Okay, all right, I get your point," I said. "If you'll let me have a turn now, maybe you'll get something that satisfies you. First, I apologize for not calling you earlier this morning. I know you're on deadline and that you get to work at an inhuman hour of the morning. End of apology. It's true that we sprung Milner; Parker got him out yesterday afternoon. Wolfe's convinced he didn't kill Stevens, and we're continuing the investigation for our client, Miss Maria Radovich." Following my instructions from last night, I gave Lon a few more sentences, including a couple of quotes from Wolfe. It was enough for a solid second-day lead on the story. Of course Lon also wanted to know where Milner was, and I suggested Maria might have the answer. "But we can't find her, either," he complained. "Where've you got them stashed?"

"You already have yourself a good story," I said. "And by the way, if you're planning to use our pictures again, I've got some more recent ones here of both

Wolfe and me. If you send a messenger over, I'll have them ready."

Lon's response also would have made Fritz blush, and he hung up before I was able to tell him the rest of my instructions under "one" were to talk only to the *Gazette*. As I walked back to the kitchen to inform Fritz that I wasn't home to any reporters, the phone rang again. When I got there, he'd already answered. "It's for Mr. Wolfe," he whispered. "A man named Remmers."

I shook my head and blinked. My second notebook item was to call Jason Remmers. I did an about-face to the office. "Keep breakfast warm," I said over my shoulder. "I'd like to eat it before lunch.

"Nero Wolfe's office, Archie Goodwin speaking," I said into the receiver.

"Yes, Mr. Goodwin," came the deep response, "this is Jason Remmers of the New York Symphony. Is Mr. Wolfe in?"

"I'm sorry, but he's not available right now. However, I can speak for him. And coincidentally, I was going to call you this morning."

"Oh?" Remmers said. "Well, I'm aware from the papers that Mr. Wolfe has a strong interest in the death of Mr. Stevens, and I was hoping to make an appointment to see him today."

"Precisely what I was going to talk to you about. Mr. Wolfe would like to see you, too. And as you may be aware, he doesn't leave his office on business. Would it be possible for you to be here this morning? Say, at eleven-fifteen?"

"Yes, that would be no problem at all. I assume your address is correct as shown in the directory?" I said it was and hung up, leaning back and staring at the ceiling. It was only nine o'clock, and already I was batting two-for-two on the day's instructions. Or was it zero-for-two? I hadn't done a damn thing so far except answer calls. Maybe our strategy should be just to sit and wait for the phone to ring.

I called Wolfe in the plant rooms.

"Well?" He always sounds disgusted when he's interrupted up there.

"Just reporting in. I've talked to Cohen, and Remmers will be here at eleven-fifteen."

"Satisfactory," he growled, hanging the phone up harder than he needed to.

I went back to the kitchen and had at least five bites of breakfast before the doorbell rang. "Whoever it is, tell them there's nobody home," I said to Fritz. "Tell them Wolfe and I have quit because of the pressure and have started a mink ranch up in Nova Scotia. Tell them anything that comes into your mind."

He disappeared down the hall and was back a few moments later. "Archie, it is Inspector Cramer. I didn't open the door, but he looks very determined."

I pushed the plate of sausage links and buckwheat cakes away. "Fritz, this wasn't meant to be eaten. Okay, I'll go and try to handle the inspector. But I'm still not home to any reporters."

Through the one-way panel, I could see that Cramer indeed looked determined. I cracked the door as far as the chain allowed. "We're not open for business yet," I said through the opening.

"Balls!" Cramer shot back. "I know Wolfe's up playing with his flowers, but you'll do. This is important."

"I'm flattered you'd come all the way up here to see me," I said, swinging open the door. With his usual manners, Cramer brushed by me and into the office without bothering to take his overcoat off, and he headed straight for the red leather chair. I followed and, since my own desk is across the room from where he'd plopped down, I sat behind Wolfe's. "I'm only half his weight," I conceded, "but this chair has strange and wondrous powers. Whenever I sit in it, I feel transformed, as if all the truths of the universe are within my grasp."

"I know I've said it before, but by God, you'll clown your way to the grave," Cramer snarled, jamming an unlit cigar into his mouth. "Listen, Archie, this is serious, or I wouldn't be here." Whenever he calls me Archie, I know he's being earnest, or making a pretense of it, so I put on a somber face.

Cramer leaned forward, resting an elbow on the corner of the desk. "Now, I know Wolfe got Milner out on bond—don't interrupt. Parker won't tell us anything more than that he's representing Milner, and that's his right, but I know damn well that whenever I find Nathaniel Parker involved in anything big in this town, Wolfe's there as well. Okay, so Milner's out, and that's his right, too. I don't know what Wolfe's game is, but I'll tell you this, Archie: He's playing with a loaded grenade this time." Cramer jabbed a finger in my direction and went on. "We've got Milner cold, and if Wolfe's trying to drum up business by convincing that Radovich girl that somebody else did it—"

"Come on, Inspector. I know you and Mr. Wolfe have gone to the mat plenty through the years, and that you've accused each other of everything from incompetence and bad faith to high treason and murder, but he has never tried to manufacture business without a solid reason, and you know it. The problem is that you've got a weak suspect."

"Weak?" Cramer slapped the arm of his chair. "Point one," he said, holding out a finger. "Milner and Stevens got into it over Maria Radovich backstage at the concert hall. Half a dozen people heard it, and they all say Stevens insulted and humiliated Milner. Point two, Milner was the only person who entered Stevens's apartment the night of the murder—he was positively identified by the hallman. Point three, we found Milner's prints four places in the apartment, including the library. Point four, Milner admits he was in the apartment. And point five, he has no alibi whatever for his whereabouts at any time during the evening of the murder, up to the moment my men arrested him coming home to his place in Queens. And you call that weak?"

"Did you find his prints on those notes Stevens got?" I asked.

"No, although everybody else's were on them," Cramer said with a scowl. "Stevens's own, of course, and Maria Radovich's—and yours. But he probably had the presence of mind to wear gloves when he printed them."

"But he didn't have the presence of mind to wear gloves in Stevens's apartment?"

"I can't answer for his actions," Cramer said, raising his voice, "but I do know there's enough on him now to put him away. I also know the pressure to clean up the case is coming all the way from Albany, and if Wolfe gets the least bit out of line on this one, his license is gone like that." Cramer snapped his fingers. "And yours too. You damn near lost it on the Cather thing, you know. Someday I'll tell you why you didn't.

"Look, Archie"—Cramer leaned forward and lowered his voice—"I like you, in spite of everything in the past. And I even kind of like Wolfe, although I can't talk to him without blowing up; that's why I came at this hour. I can reason with you—at least I think I can. I'm telling you that the commissioner and the D.A. are really watching Wolfe on this one. They'd like nothing better than an excuse to lift his license. As a friend, I'm asking you to talk Wolfe out of going on with this. Yeah, I know you'll say you don't have any influence over him, but we both know damn well that he listens to you. Don't let him make a fool of himself on this one."

"Inspector, as a friend I'm telling you that even if I did have the kind of influence over Wolfe you think I do, I wouldn't try to whistle him off, and for a very simple reason: I don't think Gerald Milner killed Stevens either."

Cramer stood up and threw his cigar at the wastebasket. It went in for the first time I can remember, and he headed for the hall. "I tried," he said as he opened the front door. "Just don't say I didn't try." I started to answer, but he'd already slammed the door, and by the time I looked through the panel, he was climbing into the unmarked car that had been waiting at the curb.

12

I finally did get through breakfast and the *Times*, but didn't have much time for general housekeeping chores in the office before Wolfe came down. By eleven-oh-one, though, when I heard the sound of the elevator, I had managed to dust, empty wastebaskets, and make a little progress on the germination records.

"We had a visitor after I talked to you on the house phone," I told Wolfe when he was settled in the chair that I had occupied an hour earlier. His face asked the question. "Inspector Cramer popped in to wish us a pleasant day," I went on. "Actually, he wasn't as interested in our having a nice day as he was that we quit the case. Seems the drive to get this one cleaned up fast is coming from all quarters, including the governor's office. If you want it verbatim, I can just about work it in before Remmers arrives," I said, looking at my watch.

"No, just the essentials," Wolfe said, riffling through the stack of mail I'd put on his blotter. I fed it to him fast, including Cramer's hint that he'd saved our licenses in the Cather mess. There was nothing in the mail to hold his interest, so Wolfe leaned back and closed his eyes during my recitation, grimacing occasionally at a comment of Cramer's.

"Pfui," he said when I was finished. "Mr. Cramer obviously came here at the insistence of others, probably the commissioner or the district attorney. It wasn't a fishing expedition, since the inspector didn't seem interested in any other suspects we might have. They're putting all their chips on Mr. Milner, to use one of your phrases. And they don't want—" The doorbell rang.

"He's sure prompt," I said, nodding toward the wall clock, which read eleven-fifteen. "By the way," I added, clearing my throat, "you should know that I didn't call Remmers—he called us. He wanted to see you."

"Indeed. Bring him in."

Standing on the stoop, Jason Remmers looked just like his pictures on the society pages—tall, at least six-three, lean, long-faced, and very, very distinguished. "Mr. Remmers," I said, opening the door, "I'm Archie Goodwin. Please come in."

"Thank you," he said, offering a large hand with a strong grip. I took his homburg and black cashmere overcoat in the front hall and ushered him into the office. "Mr. Wolfe, Mr. Remmers," I said. Wolfe stayed seated, nodding his head, and Remmers, apparently aware of his host's aversion to handshakes, didn't offer a paw. "It's a privilege to meet you, Mr. Wolfe," he said in his baritone. "I've read and heard so much about you and this office. I never thought I'd get here, and I only wish the circumstances were more pleasant," he said, settling into the red leather chair.

"Unfortunately," Wolfe said, "most of the people who come here do so because of less-than-happy circumstances. I understand that you had wanted to see me?"

Remmers crossed one long leg over the other and fingered a cuff of his six-hundred-dollar custom-made gray pinstripe. "Yes, as I told Mr. Goodwin on the telephone, I've learned from the papers that you're interested in Milan Stevens's murder. Also, my friend Mr. Bristol, the police commissioner, told me last night that you posted the bond for Gerald Milner."

"That's not technically correct," Wolfe said. "Mr. Milner's bond was posted by an attorney named Nathaniel Parker."

Remmers nodded and smiled. "All right; I've heard about your fondness for precise speech. In any event, Mr. Bristol led me to believe that you were instrumental in getting Milner released."

"That's only conjecture on the commissioner's part," Wolfe said. "Assuming it to be true, however, why are you here? Did Mr. Bristol ask you to come and dissuade us from further investigation?"

Remmers's face showed surprise. "Why, yes, as a matter of fact, he did. But that's not why I came. I'm chairman of the Symphony, and as you might imagine, these last two days have been sad and traumatic for everyone connected with the orchestra. They have been particularly so for me, as I was the one most responsible for Mr. Stevens coming to the Symphony."

Remmers paused and looked at Wolfe, who nodded slightly. "Anyway, despite the police feeling that they've found the murderer, I'm not convinced—and I told Dick Bristol as much. Perhaps Mr. Milner is the guilty one, although that would surprise me greatly. I'd feel much more comfortable if you, as well as the police, arrived at that conclusion." Remmers leaned forward in the chair. "Mr. Wolfe, all this is a long-winded way of saying I want to hire you to investigate the murder, regardless of how the commissioner feels about it. I know your fees are high, but I'm prepared to entertain any reasonable amount. I, not the Symphony, would be paying you."

"Mr. Remmers, as you would learn if you were to read the edition of the *Gazette* that will soon be on the streets, I already have a client in this case, Maria Radovich."

"Yes, Bristol seemed to be aware of that when I talked to him last night. But I'm sure I can pay a higher fee than she; or, if you prefer, perhaps an arrangement can be worked out for us to become co-clients."

Wolfe shook his head. "No, sir, that wouldn't work, and you know it. In the first place, your interests and Miss Radovich's may not totally coincide. Second, in the course of my investigation, I may uncover information detrimental either to you or to the orchestra."

"Such as?" Remmers said with a slight smile.

"It may be that you are the murderer," Wolfe said.

Remmers didn't blink. "If I were, I would hardly be trying to hire the most astute detective in New York, would I?"

"There's precedent for such a move," Wolfe answered. "Some years ago, a man engaged Mr. Goodwin and me to find out who killed an employee of the firm of which he was an officer. I found the murderer—it was our client."

"Yes, now that you mention it, I recall the case. In any event, I'm sure I'm not as clever as that murderer probably was, but I guess I see your point. And the important thing to me is that you *are* working on the murder. I can promise you full cooperation from the Symphony, at least as far as my authority extends."

Wolfe nodded. "Now we come to the reason why I had also wanted to see you, sir. I was going to request just such cooperation. For starters, you said you weren't convinced of Mr. Milner's guilt. Why?"

Remmers considered the question. "I admit I don't know Gerald Milner awfully well—he's only been with the Symphony a couple of years or so. But I've talked to him on occasion at receptions and such—I try to make it a point to meet everyone in the orchestra—and it's difficult for me to picture him being even the least bit scheming, let alone violent. The orchestra is made up of a great many disparate personalities, as you can appreciate, and his is among the mildest—perhaps 'meekest' is a better word—of them all."

"The meek and mild have wreaked a great deal of destruction through the ages," Wolfe said.

"Certainly, and it may indeed be that Milner is one of those," Remmers conceded. "But I simply don't believe it."

"Do you have someone else to suggest?"

"I've been doing a lot of thinking about it. There were a number of people who found it, well . . . *difficult* to get along with Milan Stevens. He was rigid and unbending, as you probably have heard, and a lot of people who had to work with him were put off by his attitude and personality."

"Including you?"

"I guess I was a special case. I brought him here from London two years ago—two-and-a-half, actually—and he felt a debt to me because of that. Besides, as chairman I don't get very involved in the day-to-day operations of the orchestra, so Stevens and I didn't really have occasion to clash."

"But he collided with others at a high level?"

Remmers smiled ruefully. "Yes, indeed. For instance, he and Charles Meyerhoff, the managing director, were openly hostile to each other. Charlie felt the orchestra's morale was even worse than it had been under the previous conductor, and that the choice of repertoire made us seem like a glorified Boston Pops."

Wolfe looked puzzled, and Remmers picked up on it. "That is, under Stevens, the Symphony was playing music that appealed to the greatest numbers, rather than music that was necessarily of the highest caliber, or music that was more adventuresome."

"Was this true?"

"That's a subjective judgment," Remmers answered, "although there's no question that the Symphony programs the last two seasons have run more heavily toward Tchaikovsky, Rachmaninoff, Beethoven, Brahms, and so forth, the popular composers."

"Did you agree with Mr. Meyerhoff's position on the orchestra's morale?" Wolfe asked.

"Not at first," Remmers said. "Charlie tends to be a griper by nature—never satisfied, never happy. So when he initially came to me complaining about Stevens's Prussian approach, I shrugged it off as just another example of his pessimistic outlook. Besides, one of the big reasons we brought Milan in was to reestablish discipline in the orchestra. For a number of years, the Symphony had been without a strong music director, and this was reflected in the quality of the playing. At first, I was delighted to hear about the new strictness."

"But your opinion changed?"

"Yes," Remmers said. "After the first year, I began to realize that Milan was alienating a number of people with his approach, and during the second year, it seemed as if almost everyone was being alienated by his policies, his brusqueness, his inflexibility."

"Did you talk to him about this?" Wolfe asked.

"Lord, yes, numerous times. I tried to explain that we needed discipline without intimidation, and he would always insist that this was his way of operating, that it had been successful in London, Vienna, and other places. But each time, our conversations ended with him saying he would try to be more understanding and easier to get along with.

"Unfortunately, his good intentions never seemed to last long, and Meyerhoff would be back griping to me. In the last few months, Charlie started saying he was going to quit, that he couldn't take the fighting and tension and what he felt was the overpopularization of the repertoire. He said he couldn't function when we had a music director who wanted to be the general manager as well."

"But you were able to keep Mr. Meyerhoff in the fold?" Wolfe asked.

"Barely. For the last eight months or so, my main function has been peacemaker, rather than fund-raiser and civic representative of the Symphony, which is what I'm supposed to be. It's been rough," he said, running a hand across his chin.

"Are you suggesting by all this that Mr. Meyerhoff might have killed Milan Stevens?"

Remmers jerked upright. "Oh no, no, not necessarily. There were others who probably disliked Milan every bit as much as he did. To name two, Dave Hirsch, the associate conductor, and Donald Sommers, the principal flutist."

Wolfe shifted uneasily. He hadn't rung for beer, and I knew why. "What were the causes of their animus toward Mr. Stevens?"

"Well, Hirsch had been associate conductor under the previous music director and seemed to think he was the logical choice at the time we brought in Stevens. But it was explained to him that he wasn't even being considered for the post. Off the record, he just hasn't got the presence or the depth for the job. Anyway, he's resented Stevens from day one, and it's gotten worse. Milan didn't delegate much responsibility, so Hirsch was doing less than he had before. And to make matters worse, Hirsch had composed a symphony that he would dearly love to have premiered by the orchestra. But Stevens told him he didn't find its caliber high enough for the Symphony. Since then, they've barely been on speaking terms. I've been expecting Hirsch to come in any day and tell me he's quitting after the current season."

"With Mr. Stevens dead, will Mr. Hirsch become the music director?" Wolfe asked.

Remmers shook his head vigorously. "Only on an interim basis. We're making the formal announcement of his appointment this afternoon. I've already talked to Dave, and he seems resigned to never being the Symphony's chief conductor. Down deep, I think he's aware of his limitations, and he knows he could never handle the job in the long run. I suspect he realizes that any potential he has for growth in the music world is as a composer rather than a conductor.

"In fact, part of my peacemaking work in the last few weeks was trying to persuade Stevens to give the premiere of Hirsch's symphony. And I think I just about talked him into it."

Wolfe considered the wall clock, then looked back at Remmers. "And what of Mr. Sommers?"

"Ah yes, another case of bitterness," he said. "Don Sommers performed a flute solo a few weeks ago that got so-so reviews, and not long afterward, in an interview in the *Times*, Stevens said one of his biggest problems was the lackadaisical attitude of a number of the principal players. Sommers chose to interpret this as a direct slap at him, although in the paper Stevens was quoted as criticizing 'several soloists.' Anyway, the two of them got into a shouting session backstage a day or two later, and since then, they hadn't been on speaking terms."

Wolfe frowned. "It would seem that the orchestra exists on a continuum of screaming matches and angry silences."

Remmers threw back his head and laughed. "Based on what I've told you, that's a natural enough conclusion. Actually, though, things aren't nearly that chaotic most of the time. But then, you asked specifically about those people who had problems with Milan Stevens, so you're hearing about the turmoil."

"What I started out asking for," Wolfe corrected, "were your suggestions as to who might have killed Mr. Stevens. Do you think any of the three you named—or anyone else within the orchestra—is a likely candidate?"

"A few days ago, I would have laughed off that question. But a few days ago, I'd also have scoffed at anyone who said that our music director would be stabbed to death in his own home. To be totally candid, I wouldn't rule out any of them, although I wouldn't presume to point at one as a more likely suspect than the other two. As far as the rest of the orchestra . . . no, these three and Milner were the only ones I'm aware of who've had particularly bitter experiences with Stevens."

Wolfe scowled. "Let's return to you, sir. Because you were instrumental in the hiring of Mr. Stevens, has some of the criticism of his performance been directed to you?"

"Indeed it has," Remmers said. "One paper's music critic has said that the blame for what he called the 'Stevens debacle' should rest with me. You see, at the time we were looking for a new music director, the music-policy committee was terribly split on candidates for the job. Meyerhoff is head of that committee, but they were going nowhere, so I stepped in with Stevens's name. I got support for him from committee members, and finally Meyerhoff gave in too. In recent months, some of the same people on the committee who applauded that selection began saying I made a first-class blunder."

"What has your response been to this criticism?"

"I'm pretty thick-skinned, Mr. Wolfe," he said, coming on again with that engaging grin that you see in society-page photographs. "I've been involved in a number of civic projects through the years, and I've taken a lot of shots from a lot of people because of various decisions of mine. All of which has helped me grow a tough hide. The only thing that's bothered me about the flap over Stevens is the realization I've come to in the last six months: Stevens wasn't working out. I *had* made a bum call, and I was prepared to rectify it."

"Were you planning to fire him?" Wolfe asked.

"In effect. His contract was up for renewal, and I was going before the board with the suggestion that we seek a new music director."

"Was Mr. Stevens aware of this?"

"I hadn't talked to him about it, although I would have in the next few weeks," Remmers said. "I think he probably suspected it might be coming, though."

"Would you have taken this as a personal failure?" Wolfe asked.

Remmers shrugged his lean shoulders. "Not really. Again, I'm used to criticism—you can't have a position like this one without being a target. And considering the problems the Symphony had with its last few conductors, Stevens really wasn't that much of a disaster."

"Mr. Remmers, if I may shift to another subject," Wolfe said, "do you know a woman named Lucinda Forrester-Moore?"

"I suppose you could say I know her," Remmers said. "I've met her at a number of parties, benefits, that sort of thing, through the years. Her late husband, Baxter Moore, and I both went to Harvard, and we ran into each other at alumni functions; he was in the shipping business. I guess I know why you're asking about her: She and Milan Stevens had become an item in the last year or so."

"Did you perceive theirs as a serious relationship?" Wolfe asked.

"I couldn't really say. They were together a good deal, of course, but I could never figure out whether it was romantic or just a handy pairing. Lucinda loves to be in the middle of things, and it's pretty damn presti-

gious to have the Symphony maestro on your arm
when you sweep into the theater or a dinner party. But
then, since her husband's death six, seven years ago,
she's had a history of attracting well-known men—it's
sort of her trademark."

"Did Mr. Stevens ever mention her to you?"

"No, I don't think so," Remmers said. "However,
there was no particular reason why he should. Our own
relationship wasn't such that personal matters were discussed. In fact, I can't picture Milan Stevens discussing
his personal life with anybody."

Wolfe drew in half the oxygen in the room, then
exhaled slowly. "Just two more questions, Mr. Remmers.
First, if I want to see the three men you mentioned,
could you arrange it?"

"Yes, I think so. You'd want to see them here, of
course. They might not like it, particularly Charlie
Meyerhoff, but they'll come, either together or sepa-
rately, as you wish. If you let me know when you want
them . . ."

"Mr. Goodwin will call you with a precise time," Wolfe
said. "And we'll want to see them all at once. The other
question, sir: Where were you on Wednesday night
between seven-thirty and eight-thirty?"

Remmers flashed that grin again. It was easy to see
him in the role of fund-raiser. "I knew that was coming. Nineteen nights out of twenty, I'd have a drum-
tight alibi—a dinner, a reception, the opera, maybe the
Symphony itself. But I had an upset stomach Wednesday, so I begged off a dinner invitation at the home of
some friends, and my wife went alone. I spent the early
part of the evening reading, and about a quarter to
eight, I went out for a walk—I needed the fresh air to
help settle me. I walked around a few blocks in our
neighborhood—we live on Beekman Place—and I was
back home by nine or so. Unfortunate timing, isn't it?"

"Did you see anyone?" Wolfe asked.

"Just the doorman in our building, and I suppose the hallman, too. The doorman and I chatted briefly both when I left and came back. Otherwise, I saw at least a dozen people walking their dogs, but nobody I knew."

"Very well," Wolfe said, looking at the wall clock again. "I know your schedule is a busy one, and I appreciate your taking the time to come here."

"Thank *you*, Mr. Wolfe," Remmers said, rising. He started to reach out a hand, then remembered where he was and dipped his head. I followed him out to the front hall and helped him on with the cashmere, then watched him bound down the steps to a parked limousine that looked to be twice the length of the car that had waited for Cramer earlier.

When I got back to the office, Fritz was on his way out, having just deposited a glass and two bottles of beer in front of Wolfe. "Hah!" I said. "You didn't want him to see you drinking the family brew, did you? Afraid he'd think you were buttering him up?"

"Nonsense," Wolfe shot back as he poured beer and watched the foam settle. "It merely would have distracted from our conversation. Mr. Remmers undoubtedly would have felt some comment was necessary, which in turn would have elicited a response from me, and so on. I did not invite him here to indulge in small talk."

"You didn't invite him at all, he invited himself," I retorted, but his face was already hidden by an open book, which always happens when I get in the last word.

13

I'm sure Fritz's poached salmon with mousseline d'homard was superb, but for the third straight day I was eating without tasting. I envy Wolfe's facility for totally shutting out business whenever he crosses the sill into the dining room; that afternoon he put away three big helpings of the salmon, all the while holding forth on how future historians might view the presidency of one Richard M. Nixon. I threw in a few comments here and there, but on balance I was hardly a good conversational partner. As strong as my own feelings are about the man from San Clemente, I couldn't get my mind off Maria Radovich and Jason Remmers and Gerald Milner, the last of whom was at that very moment sitting in the South Room eating the same food we were.

It seemed as if lunch lasted six hours, but finally we were back in the office with coffee, which meant business was fair game again. "Look," I said, swiveling in my chair to face Wolfe, "how long are we going to keep our houseguest? I can't see that he's doing us any good here."

Wolfe sipped his coffee and set the cup down deliberately. "I agree that the time has come to turn Mr. Milner loose. My principal reason for housing him was to give Mr. Cohen and his newspaper an advantage over their competition on the story. They now have that advantage, so he should be told that he is free to go."

What Wolfe was actually saying was that I should suggest to Milner that he pack. Heaven forbid that Wolfe himself have to tell a guest to leave. I was about to make a remark when the doorbell rang.

"Probably Cramer," I said, "back again to try talking us off the case. Are you available?"

He grunted. "Yes, I'll see him."

But it wasn't the inspector's mug I saw when I looked through the one-way panel. I wouldn't have wanted to try guessing her age, although her well-coiffed white hair told me she'd already been around awhile when I first saw the light of day back in Ohio. Her skin looked as good as a teenager's, though, and if pressed for a single adjective, I would have called her elegant. She was wearing a black coat with a white fur collar that had to have set her back a few bills. Whoever she was, I concluded she was no immediate threat, so I slid off the chain lock.

"Yes?" I said, swinging open the door.

"I would like to see Mr. Wolfe," she said. "I realize I don't have an appointment, but I know he is at home most of the time." Her voice seemed tinged with French, although as Wolfe has pointed out a number of times, I'm out of my league when it comes to languages and accents.

"I don't know if he can be disturbed right now," I said, stepping back and letting her in so I could close the door against the November gusts. "I'll ask, though. Who should I say is calling?"

"My name is Alexandra Adjari," she said.

It registered, of course, and I turned toward the open door to the office. When I got there, Wolfe was on his feet, looking past me into the hall with an expression I'd never seen him wear. I was trying to read it when she eased past me. "Hello, Nero, it's been a long time," she said, holding out a gloved hand.

"Alexandra," he answered, shaking hands across the desk. "I recognized your voice instantly."

"Even though you hadn't heard it in heaven knows how many years?" she said with a laugh. A nice laugh. "I don't believe you, Nero, but thank you for saying it. You're looking well."

Wolfe gestured at himself. "As you can see, I've added layers through the years—insulation against life's myriad assaults." He turned toward me. "This is Mr. Goodwin."

She took my hand with a firm grasp and smiled. "I assumed so when I saw him at the door. I've read a good deal about both of you through the years. I see the New York *Times* frequently."

Wolfe dipped his head a full inch, which is for him a sweeping bow. "Please," he said, indicating the red leather chair. I took her coat and hung it up, and when I got back, he was asking if she'd eaten.

"Yes, thank you, I had lunch on the plane coming over. I've only just been in New York an hour or so. I started making arrangements to come as soon as I heard about Milos. As you can imagine, it's big news in London, too."

Wolfe nodded, and at his suggestion, Alexandra agreed to have coffee. After Fritz had served her and she'd taken a first sip, he readjusted himself and dabbed the corner of his mouth with a handkerchief. "You've come for the memorial services?"

"Partly," she said, "but also to be with Maria Radovich. I'm very fond of her, and I thought she might need some comforting, having no relatives other than Milos. I tried to call her after I checked in at the Churchill, but there was no answer at their apartment."

"Mr. Goodwin knows her whereabouts," Wolfe said, "and can tell you how to reach her. I can assure you she's in the care of friendly and sympathetic persons. As far as memorial arrangements, details are not yet firm."

Alexandra waved her hand. "That's not my main concern," she said. "Let the dead bury their dead. I know that must sound callous, considering that I was married to the man for seventeen years, but as I think you know, it was a marriage in name only after the first three years or so. We were separated the rest of the time, and we were divorced . . ."—she paused to think— ". . . more years ago than I care to remember. I don't think I've even seen Milos more than four or five times in all the years since then. I can still remember what you told me after I decided to marry him—can you?"

Wolfe nodded and took another sip of coffee.

She went on. "You said we wouldn't last five years together, and that I should reconsider. In the early months after the wedding, I laughed to myself about that, thinking how wrong you were. But by the end of that first year, I knew what a mistake we'd made, how totally unsuited we were to each other. When I was with him constantly over a long period of time, I found that Milos was hard to love, harder still to like. Fortunately, his music took him away so frequently that we stayed together longer than we would have otherwise. Even at that, the marriage was an almost total disaster. The only good things I can think of were that we didn't have any children and that because of Milos, I came to know Maria."

She paused for some coffee. "Long after we divorced, Milos came to London as conductor of the Philharmonia, and I met him at a reception. We were polite to each other, and he introduced me to Maria, who was then about thirteen. I liked her right away, and she seemed fond of me, too. I know Milos tried to discourage her from being friendly with me, at least at first, but Maria has her own mind, and we grew close over the next several years. Since she moved here with Milos, we write to each other only occasionally, but I still think of her often. It's because of Maria that I came. Now that I'm here, though, I find another purpose: In my room at the hotel was a copy of today's New York *Gazette,* and it said that you're investigating Milos's murder, that you're not satisfied the right man has been arrested. Is that correct?"

"It is," Wolfe said.

"The newspaper also said you're acting on Maria's behalf."

"Also true," Wolfe said. "I'm sure she'll tell you as much when you meet."

"I have never met her beau, of course, but I suppose it's natural she would think him innocent. You must also be convinced of his innocence." It was a statement, not a question.

"I am," Wolfe said, "although I can offer no other candidate at the present time."

"I'm sure your reasons are good. I know Maria has limited funds of her own, at least until the estate is settled, but I have no such constraint. Nero, I want to employ you to find Milos's murderer, and you may set whatever fee you wish."

I looked at Wolfe. We already had a client, albeit one whose assets would hardly qualify her as a preferred customer at Metropolitan Trust. But in the last few hours, two heavy hitters had stepped up and asked to join the team. I waited for his answer, although I knew what it would be.

"I appreciate the offer, but—"

"I know, you're wondering why I would do this for a

man for whom I had no feelings all these years. I suppose it's because of Maria, and because he *was* my husband once. And perhaps because of my own conscience. I was as much the cause of the marriage's failure as he."

"What I started to say," Wolfe replied, "was that I appreciate the offer, but even Miss Radovich is only a token client. As you well know, I owe Milos Stefanovic my life."

She nodded and looked thoughtful. "Yes, that day in Cetinje, the police, the blockade . . ."

"I was a consummate fool," Wolfe said. "I made every possible mistake, but Milos appeared from somewhere with a rifle and a pistol. He must have killed three of them."

"Five, he said, when he told me the story later. But I seem to recall that you saved him at least once also, Nero."

Wolfe turned a palm over. "I suppose one could say we all saved each other on numerous occasions. But nothing as marked as what happened that afternoon. It is a debt, and I dislike being in debt."

"You've changed very little," Alexandra said, smiling again. "Even then, you hated owing anything to anyone. Well, if you won't take my money, you certainly have my moral support, for what that's worth."

"Thank you," Wolfe said, bowing again. I was beginning to get worried about him. Three times this week he had stood when women entered or left the office, if you count twice for Maria, and I'd lost track of the number of times he'd bowed. If this trend kept up, he'd soon start helping women on with their coats or opening the front door for them.

"Nero," Alexandra said, "I've come to New York a number of times through the years, and I've often thought of calling or stopping by. For some reason, I never did, but I always told myself I would one day.

And I promised myself that when I did, I would ask to see those famous orchids. Is that presumptuous?"

Wolfe raised his eyebrows. "Presumptuous? Quite the contrary. Mr. Goodwin will tell you that I rarely deny that request. If you feel rested, we can go now," he said, lifting himself from the chair.

"I certainly do," she replied, and they made for the hall. "You'll stay for dinner, of course," Wolfe asked.

"I'd like that, if it's no imposition," Alexandra replied.

"In this house, a meal is always—" The rest of Wolfe's sentence was chopped off by the closing of the elevator door.

I sat back down in my chair and stared at the wall. She and Wolfe went back a long way, and the relationship obviously hadn't been a casual one. Well, I'll be damned, I said to myself, or maybe it was out loud. I thought I had long ago learned everything I was going to know about Nero Wolfe, but here was something new. I smiled and started in on some of the office work that had been piling up.

I'd been at it about ten minutes when the phone rang. It was Wolfe, from the plant rooms. "I wanted to remind you that Mr. Milner is free to go, and indeed, he'd probably like to leave soon so he can visit Miss Radovich. Also, I know you see Saul regularly to play cards. What about Fred—is he still working?"

"Yes, or at least he's trying. Bascomb uses him once in a while, but I know things have been slow for him."

"Can you have both of them here tomorrow, say, at eleven?"

"I can certainly try," I said. "And by the way, I may have forgotten to mention that I'm dining at Miss Rowan's tonight."

"Satisfactory," he said, hanging up.

I allowed myself another grin. You may think the "satisfactory" was in response to my trying to deliver a pair of men to the office the next morning, but it was really his reaction to knowing there would be only two at the dinner table in the brownstone. And for the record, I didn't have a date at Lily Rowan's, although I was pretty sure I could wangle one. While I was at it, maybe I could hook an invite for Milner as well, since there was a certain party at Lily's that he wanted to see. I turned back to the phone.

14

At eleven o'clock on Saturday morning, Nero Wolfe stepped out of the elevator that had lowered him from the plant rooms and walked into his office to find the three of us waiting: Saul Panzer in the red leather chair, Fred Durkin in one of the yellow chairs, me at my desk. They stood when he came in, and he stopped to shake hands with both of them—something he reserves for perhaps a dozen men. He then circled behind his desk, sat, and rang for beer.

Pretty cool, I thought. He hasn't seen them in close to two years, but he's acting like they were over for dinner yesterday. In case you're new in these precincts, Saul and Fred were free-lancing for Wolfe long before the Giants and Dodgers snuck off to California. About Saul Panzer: He's short, his face is mostly nose, his clothes are rumpled, and he always looks like he hasn't shaved for three days, although he insists he takes a blade to his mug every morning. But he's hands down the finest operative, free-lance or otherwise, in the city of New York, when it comes to tailing someone or sniffing out clues or persuading people to spit out information they'd rather keep to themselves. Saul asks for, and gets, double the going rate, and he never hurts for business, although through the years he's always been willing to rearrange his schedule for Wolfe.

Fred Durkin is a big guy, thick at the waist, thick at the neck, and maybe a little thick upstairs, too, although he's almost as good as Saul at tailing, and he's as honest and loyal as you'll ever find. But as I had told Wolfe, Fred wasn't getting much work these days. Fortunately, his wife, Fanny, had a job at a branch library someplace out on Long Island, so at least a little money was coming in.

But I've gotten a bit ahead of myself, so I'll back up to yesterday afternoon. The moment Wolfe and Alexandra went up to the plant rooms, I was on the phone. I got Saul on the first try, which surprised me, and when I told him Wolfe wanted to see him, he said: "The Stevens thing; I'll be there." That's Saul. Fred was home too, and from the tone of his voice, I knew he'd crawl across Manhattan for a job, especially with Wolfe. He'd be there too. Next came a call to Lily. I landed that dinner invitation, all right, for both Milner and me, so his short stay as our houseguest was over, and I could have back the clothes of mine that he'd been wearing for the last day or so, and which were about two sizes too large for him. Actually, he hadn't been much of an imposition to us, as he'd almost never come out of the South Room, which may be a tribute to the high quality of the books on the shelves up there.

As he and I rode to Lily's in a cab, Milner was quiet but didn't seem terribly worried, or terribly curious about our progress, for that matter. When I asked why, he said, "I didn't do it, and I know Mr. Wolfe's reputation. I'm just thankful he's working on this, because I know he'll find the right one." I wish I were that confident, I thought, slouching in the seat and staring out at the snowflakes swirling in the wind.

Maria was still staying at Lily's, and she seemed brightened by Milner's appearance, although she was preoccupied with plans for a memorial service for her uncle, which was set for Monday. She brightened further when I told her Alexandra Adjari was in town and would be calling her either that night or the next morning. As it turned out, Alexandra went one better, stopping off at Lily's about ten-thirty on her way from the brownstone to her hotel, and the two had a tears-and-hugs reunion right there in the living room. It ended up with Alexandra insisting that Maria stay with her at the Churchill, which meant Lily was losing her houseguest, too. The two women and Milner left in a cab—he had decided to go back to his apartment in Queens—and all of a sudden, Lily and I had her palace to ourselves. That's a whole story in itself, and not for these pages, but now you're up-to-date on Friday night's developments.

When Fritz brought Wolfe's beer, he took orders from the rest of us: coffee for Saul and me, and beer for Fred, who doesn't like it that much but thinks he should drink it when he's with Wolfe, to be sociable. After everyone was served, Wolfe's eyes moved from Saul to Fred and back again. We were all a touch uneasy, I think, as it was the first time we'd been together in this room since Orrie had blown himself up on the front stoop. In the past, Saul, Fred, and Orrie had almost always come as a group for instructions, and the empty yellow chair was on all our minds.

Wolfe set his glass down and began: "You both read the papers regularly, so you no doubt know I'm involved in a case." They nodded. "You also know then that Milos Stefanovic, or Milan Stevens as he called himself, was a Montenegrin whom I had known many years ago in Europe. In addition, the papers have reported, correctly, that I do not believe Stefanovic was killed by Gerald Milner." Wolfe proceeded to fill them in on the last few days' activities, asking me several times to insert first-person narrative, such as when I went into the Stevens library and saw the body. When he had finished, he poured more beer and watched the foam settle. "Before the weekend is over," he said, "I hope to talk to Messrs. Meyerhoff, Hirsch, and Sommers of the Symphony, if Archie can get them here. Archie also is going to visit Mrs. Forrester-Moore at her home—she was a frequent companion of Mr. Stevens's in the last few months." I glared at Wolfe, who ignored me and went on.

"Saul, go to the building where Stevens lived. Find some pretense to get inside. I'd like to know how many entrances there are, and how easy it would be to enter and leave without being seen by the hallman. Is there a fire escape? A back stairway? A service elevator?" I smiled and bit my lip. Wolfe was out of practice, because these were questions Saul would answer without being asked. If I knew him, he'd bring back a blueprint of the whole place, complete with heating ducts and wiring.

Wolfe shifted his glance. "Fred, learn what you can about the hallman who was on duty that night, his name is—" He turned to me. "Tom Hubbard," I said. "Find out what you can about Mr. Hubbard and his habits, but don't talk to him, at least not yet. The police have surely questioned him thoroughly, and he'll be on his guard."

As Wolfe talked, Fred was scribbling in a pocket notebook, unlike Saul, who never takes any notes but keeps everything filed away upstairs. When Wolfe had finished with his briefing, the two of them got up, businesslike as usual, and shook hands again with him. It was almost like old times as I walked to the front hall with them.

"Write when you have time, even if it's only a postcard," I said as they started out the door.

"Good luck with the society doll," Saul retorted, wink-ing. "Understand she's quite a babe. Can you handle it?" I silently mouthed a word and slammed the door behind them.

Back in the office, Wolfe had picked up a book, *In Praise of English*, by Joseph T. Shipley. I sat at my desk and swiveled to face him. "Thanks so much for filling me in on my assignments," I said. "I always appreciate getting orders in front of company."

Wolfe put down the book and raised his eyebrows. "Indeed? Fred and Saul company? You're the one who once said they're part of the family, and I agree. Fur-ther, I hadn't decided who was going to do what until you were all sitting here."

"Hah! Who else but me would you send to see an attractive woman?"

He didn't reply, and I couldn't see his expression because the open book was in the way. After about five minutes, I exhaled loudly and deeply. "Okay, what do you want done first, Lucinda or the three from the Symphony?"

"Try to see the lady as soon as possible," came the voice from behind the book. "As for the others, tomor-row afternoon will be soon enough. Mr. Remmers can be of some help there."

"Any special instructions regarding the woman with the hyphenated name?" I asked.

"Use your intelligence guided by experience," Wolfe said, still behind the book. It was a favorite line of his.

"Consider it done," I said, getting up to go to the kitchen for a glass of milk. I was afraid that if I stayed in the same room with him for another thirty seconds, I might do something natural, such as braining him with his ebony paperweight.

15

I considered calling first, but decided my chances of seeing her might be better if I just showed up. I put on my best suit, a gray glen plaid, along with a light blue shirt and a blue-and-red paisley tie that Lily says makes me look debonair. Not bad, I told the mirror before giving my hair one more swipe with a brush. It was two-twenty when I grabbed my coat from the hall rack. Wolfe was back at his desk, reading. During lunch, I hadn't been very talkative, partly because I was still sore at him and partly because I was thinking about how to approach one of the town's reigning social lionesses.

Lucinda Forrester-Moore isn't listed in the Manhattan telephone directory, but Lily has some sort of guide to the city's elite, and when I called her, she looked up the address, which turned out to be a building about two blocks up Park from her own place. That was too long a walk on too cold a day, so I took a cab. The driver pulled up in front of one of those tall white modern buildings that have so many setbacks they look like squared-off wedding cakes, a style which if nothing else provides terraces for a lot of the upper-altitude apartments. A doorman who still had his uniform from Napoleon's army sniffed as I passed him, and I found myself in a circular lobby that was all floor-to-ceiling mirrors. There was an alcove at the far side of the circle where a hallman in a pretty snappy uniform of his own sat behind a desk. He looked up as I approached, but didn't open his mouth.

"I'd like to see Mrs. Forrester-Moore," I said. "My name is Archie Goodwin." I gave him my top-of-the-line calling card, a glossy eggshell-white job with my name engraved in the center and the words "Office of Nero Wolfe" in the lower right-hand corner. "Is she expecting you?" he asked in a bored tone that he probably practiced evenings at home.

"No, but I think she'll want to see me. When you call upstairs, make sure you mention that I'm from Nero Wolfe's office," I said, trying to sound bored myself.

He turned to his white telephone and punched out a number. He kept his voice so low I couldn't hear him from three feet away, and after a few seconds he hung up and turned back to me.

"She'll see you," he said, wearing the disappointment all over his face. "Sixteenth floor." He pointed to the elevators in a hallway off the circle. A young kid in a not-so-fancy uniform ran me up to sixteen in silence, and as the doors opened, he pointed to the left. "That's the door you go to," he said. "Only apartment on the floor."

When I pressed the buzzer, I didn't hear anything ring, but after a few seconds the door swung open to reveal a mousy little woman in a black-and-white uniform with a starched cap. "Mr. Goodwin?" she asked. When I nodded she slid to one side in a classic maid's motion so I could pass. I was in an entrance hall the size of a small church, with a chandelier that looked as if it could light Madison Square Garden. "Please wait in here," the maid said, leading me to a sitting room with a white rug, white walls, and white furniture. "Mrs. Forrester-Moore asked me to tell you she'll join you shortly."

"Shortly" turned out to be twenty-four minutes by the digital watch Lily had given me for my birthday. I was on the second cigarette when she walked in and held out a manicured hand. "Mr. Goodwin. This *is* a nice surprise," she said. "I hope you'll pardon the wait; I was napping when you rang and . . ." She smiled and gestured at her clothes and her hair. Even at fifty-plus, Lucinda Forrester-Moore was easy to look at. She was wearing a floor-length yellow-and-orange flowered number with ruffles on the cuffs and collar, and her dusty-blond hair looked like the handiwork of a gilt-edged Fifth Avenue salon.

"Please sit down," she said with a slight trace of some kind of accent. This was my week for foreign women. "Can I get you a drink?" she asked as she sat in a chair across the coffee table from mine.

I said no and began to state my business, when she interrupted. "I've heard and read about you before, of course, but haven't we met somewhere? I should remember, but I can't."

"You've got a good memory at that," I said with a grin. "It was several years ago, possibly at Rustermans; I was with Lily Rowan."

"Of course—Lily, now I recall it. A delightful girl. I haven't run into her for a long time. Do you still see her?"

I said I did, and that she had sent her best. All the while, I was getting a very thorough once-over.

"Mr. Goodwin, I love your suit—is it a Ralph Lauren?"

"It's a Bloomingdale's markdown," I said, "but thanks

anyway. Now, Mrs. Forrester-Moore, the reason I'm here—"

"That's such a clumsy name to say, isn't it?" she asked, flashing her pearly whites. "I wish you'd just call me Lucinda, everybody does. I was married once, but I held onto my maiden name, Forrester, too. Perhaps that was silly, but I wanted to keep part of my old self. And I'm sure I know why you're here. It's about Milan." Her expression became instantly sober. "I read that your Nero Wolfe is interested in the case, although I can't imagine why. Don't they think they've caught the murderer?"

"Mr. Wolfe isn't so sure, and because he's a genius, I take his word for things and try to humor him."

"I'd love to meet the man sometime," she said, tucking her feet under her. "But how can I be of help to you now?"

"Well, Mrs. Forrester—Lucinda—you and Mr. Stevens had been together a lot in the last few months, and I thought perhaps you might have some insight as to who might have wanted him dead."

"The police stopped by and asked me the same thing," she said, shrugging and rolling her round blue eyes. "I'll tell you what I told them: If Milan had enemies, I wasn't conscious of it. Mr. Goodwin, he was a very private person, especially about his work. He rarely talked about the orchestra when we were together, and I never brought up the subject. I think one of the reasons he enjoyed being with me was that he could escape from that part of his life completely." She accented the last word.

"I can appreciate that," I said, "but maybe without realizing it at the time, you heard a remark from Mr. Stevens or overheard something said to him that might be significant. Surely he didn't keep everything to himself."

"Oh, no, occasionally he'd bring up the Symphony,

but not often at all." She did the eye-roll again. "The only time I can remember his making a negative comment was about Mr. Remmers."

"Jason Remmers?"

"Yes, although it was just a passing remark, something about how he felt Jason was losing confidence in him. But Milan didn't seem too concerned at the time. I shouldn't have even mentioned it to you, it was so insignificant."

"How long ago was that?"

Another shrug. "Oh, maybe two or three months. Really, it was just an aside, nothing important. I'm sorry I brought it up."

"Did he ever talk about anyone else in the Symphony? Mr. Meyerhoff, perhaps. Or Gerald Milner, or—"

"No, Archie—may I call you Archie? I hate formality. No, honestly, it wasn't like him to speak about the job. He spent so much time on the orchestra as it was that he didn't like to think about it after hours." She shifted in her chair and adjusted her hem to give me a glimpse of a sandaled ankle and a trim calf. "I want as badly as you to see the murderer punished, probably worse. But why doesn't Mr. Wolfe think Gerald Milner did it?"

"Beats me. As I said before, he's a genius, and he doesn't usually share his thought processes with me. I assume you were aware that Gerald Milner and Maria Radovich were serious about each other?"

"Yes, I knew that," she said, looking down and smoothing her gown over her lap. "I had only met him once, in the lounge at Symphony Hall, I think it was. Now that you mention it, Milan *did* bring up his name once or twice, and it was obvious that he wasn't overly fond of him. He seemed like a nice young man, though, and I was shocked about . . . what has happened."

"Can you remember specifically what Stevens said about him?"

"Oh, it was something like 'I don't know how Maria could be interested in him.' Like the Remmers thing, it was just a passing comment, he didn't go on about it. When I said I thought he was nice, Milan changed the subject."

She paused and frowned. "Maybe you already know this, but Maria has never been, well, *friendly* to me. Oh, I understand why. Milan was a father to her, and I suppose she would be naturally hostile to any woman he became attracted to. About Maria—I've tried to call her several times since . . . that night, but there's always no answer. I'd like to do anything I can to help her, if she'll let me. Do you know where she is?"

"I think she's staying with some friends," I said. "If I see her, I'll tell her you've been trying to reach her. You mentioned Milan Stevens being fond of you: Did you plan to get married?"

"You ask direct questions, don't you? I suppose that's understandable in your line of work," she said with a tired smile. "Once was enough for me, Archie. I wouldn't call my marriage perfect, but my husband was a good man, and a generous provider." Her eyes moved around the room as if to underscore the statement. "We had no children, neither of us wanted any, and since I've been a widow, six years now, I find I like the freedom of living alone. I have lots of friends, lots of activities. And besides, Milan never asked me. I'm not sure he fancied the idea of getting married again either."

"If I'm not mistaken, you went out with Charles Meyerhoff at one time, too," I said.

Lucinda laughed. "You know a lot, don't you? Oh, Charles and I went to some parties and plays at one time a few years back, but it was just a thing of convenience for both of us. Nothing serious. I just like to be around people in the arts. I come from a theatrical family myself, Archie. My father was an actor back in Europe, and we lived all over the Continent when I was young. I did a little acting myself for a while, but it was only amateur things. I didn't inherit his talent, I guess. Are you sure I can't mix you a drink?"

"Thanks again, but I'd better be on my way," I said. "I appreciate the time you've taken. One more thing: Can you recall where you were Wednesday night, say, from about seven-thirty to nine?"

Another tired smile. "You have to ask that, of course, Archie. I realize you have your orders. Yes, I can remember what I did Wednesday. I knew Milan would be home working that night—he planned his schedule far in advance, even down to which nights he stayed home working on scores, and he didn't deviate from that schedule. We had been invited to a small late supper up in the Eighties—by some people named Morrison whom I've known for many years. Lawrence Morrison's in the phone directory, on East Eighty-second, if you want to check. I went alone. I think I got there about eight-thirty."

"And before that?" I asked.

"Well, at about seven I realized that I had forgotten to get flowers to take to them, so I left here early, about seven-thirty, I think, and caught a cab in front. We must have tried six or seven florists before I finally found one that stays open late. And I did end up getting a very nice arrangement."

"You wouldn't happen to remember who the florist was, would you?" I asked with a grin that was intended to show that the questions were friendly.

She fluttered a hand. "Oh, it was someplace down on Lexington, I think. Honestly, Archie, I don't remember because I stopped at so many. I'm sorry."

I couldn't see that there was anything else to talk about, so I got up to go and thanked her again. "I do wish I could be more help," she said, standing next to me and looking up with those stunning blue eyes. "While we were sitting, I didn't realize how tall you were."

There was probably a snappy retort to that line, but I couldn't think of it, so I said thanks one last time and eased my way toward the door with Lucinda at my side. She made me promise to keep her posted on developments and we said good-bye—with a handshake. Maybe it's my ego, but I had the feeling she would have preferred a more intimate parting gesture.

On the way down in the elevator and walking along Park Avenue, I tried to analyze her, and then decided I'd dump the whole thing on Wolfe, since he's the one people hire. I ruled against stopping to see Lily, and instead ducked into a drugstore with a pay phone. Jason Remmers answered himself after two rings, and I told him about Wolfe's plan for tomorrow.

"Sunday afternoon, eh?" he said after I'd laid it out. "Well, there isn't a concert, so that's no problem. I'll start calling them right now; I'm sure they're all in town, so that shouldn't give us any trouble. If I ask them to see Wolfe, they'll do it. What time?"

On Sundays, Wolfe doesn't have the usual routine, so I told him four o'clock would be fine, and Remmers said he'd call back later to let me know the outcome. Back outside, the snow had covered the sidewalk and was still falling, but I needed the air to clear away the memories of Lucinda's perfume. The walk would get me home just about the time Wolfe came down from the plant rooms.

16

In fact, it was five minutes after six when I walked into the office, and Wolfe was already behind his desk. He scowled and set his book down, knowing that I wouldn't let him get any reading done until I'd reported.

"Number one," I said, "Remmers is arranging to have the trio here tomorrow afternoon. Because you didn't give me a time, I said four. Number two, I've just been to see Lucinda the Hyphen, and her alibi for Wednesday night isn't any better than Remmers's. I assume you want it verbatim?"

Wolfe nodded and rang for beer.

"Okay, but before I start, a few observations about her," I said, "since you trust my instincts when it comes to attractive women. And she *is* an attractive woman, for sure. It's easy to see why Stevens went for her. I'm not ready to give any odds one way or the other on whether she did it, but she didn't seem terribly unhappy. No black veils or anything like that. And she made it clear that she wouldn't mind if we got to know each other better."

"Indeed? Did you find out the extent of her friendship with Mr. Stevens?"

"You said to use intelligence guided by experience, didn't you?" With that, I gave him the whole thing, word for word, although I was interrupted by two phone calls. The first was from Remmers, who reported that he had reached all three men, and they would come tomorrow at four, although he said they weren't very enthusiastic about it, particularly Hirsch and Meyerhoff. About five minutes later, Saul called and said he and Fred were ready to report. I checked with Wolfe, who said they should come after dinner. Between the calls and Wolfe's questions, it took well over an hour, so that when I was through, it was time to go into the dining room.

The shock of being back at work must have worn off, because I was beginning to appreciate Fritz again. His scallops were magnificent that night, and when Wolfe complimented him, his smile wrapped all the way around his face.

Saul and Fred timed it perfectly. We were just finishing our first cup of coffee in the office when the bell rang. I opened the door, helped them off with their coats, and told Saul that Lucinda had proposed to me. After they were settled in the office with coffee of their own, Saul cleared his throat and began.

"The building is fairly typical for the neighborhood," he said. "Nine stories, brick. I talked my way in as a Buildings Department inspector making a periodic check. I've got a card that looks good, and it usually works." I held back a smile and saw that Wolfe was doing the same; the left corner of his mouth was twitching.

"As to access," Saul continued, "there's the front door and the lobby, of course—Archie, you've seen those. In the lobby is one passenger elevator, automatic. Also, they have a service elevator and an interior fire stairway in the rear of the building. Both of them open on a small service lobby on the ground floor. That lobby" —Saul paused for a sip of coffee—"opens out onto a gangway that separates the building from the one next door. The only exit from the gangway is an iron gate seven feet high that fronts on Seventy-sixth Street to the left of the building as you face it. The gate has a panic bar on the inside, so anyone can get out by pushing it, but from the sidewalk, you can't get in without a key. The doorman on duty told me he lets tradesmen in through that gate, but only after checking with tenants to make sure they're expecting someone. He's got a key to the gate attached to his belt by a chain, and when he goes off duty, he turns it over to the doorman or hallman on the next shift."

"Is it possible to go from the gangway through to the next street?" Wolfe asked.

"Not without a ladder or wings. There's a brick wall about ten feet high that separates the property from the building behind it. I'd scratch that possibility. As to staffing, this place isn't as well covered as the big castles over on Park. There *is* a hallman on duty around the clock—that's three of them in all, in eight-hour shifts. The one you mentioned, Tom Hubbard, works four to midnight weekdays. But the building has a doorman only from six in the morning to seven at night—two men each work six-and-a-half-hour shifts. If anyone needs a taxi at any other time, the hallman has to go out and flag it."

"Anything else?" Wolfe asked.

"I'm afraid not," Saul said apologetically. "As it was, I was stretching my inspector's role. With what's happened in that building, the super and everybody else there was jumpy. I had to try to make this seem like a routine check of the exits, the stairways, what-have-you. Luckily, there hadn't been a real inspector around for a while."

"Satisfactory," Wolfe said. Saul Panzer can do no wrong as far as he's concerned, and he knew Saul always feels bad if he doesn't deliver what he thinks is one hundred and ten percent. Now it was Fred's turn, and we all shifted our attention to him.

"Well," he began in his deliberate way, "I followed your instructions, Mr. Wolfe. I didn't try to see Hubbard at all, but I did walk along the block and talk to several doormen. These guys have to all know each other, but the first couple weren't much help. One thought I was a reporter, and he wanted money before he'd tell me anything about Hubbard—I didn't know if there was anything to tell, so I said no thanks. And another one clammed up when I finally admitted to him that I was a private cop. But then something happened that was sort of interesting." Fred stopped, wrinkled his brow, and looked at Wolfe as if asking permission to go on. Wolfe dipped his head a fraction of an inch.

"Actually, it started with a coincidence," Fred said. "A doorman about six doors east of the murder building on the other side of the street is an Irishman—named Callaway. He's a talkative guy, and I struck up a conversation with him, it wasn't hard. Well, it turns out that our people come from the same county in Ireland, and possibly even the same town. Anyway, you're not interested in that, I know, but it's what got us started. Okay, after we'd been chewing for a while out in front of his building, I asked Callaway if this wasn't the block where the big murder happened. He says yes, and I begin asking, just in conversation, you know, about the building and if he knew anybody who worked over there. He tells me he doesn't think a lot of the way the place is run, that it's not well maintained, that it's got poor security, what with a doorman for only part of the time, while his building has one all night. It wasn't hard to shift the conversation to this guy Hubbard, and Callaway says he knows him. What's more, he says he hasn't got much use for him. I asked why, and he said something like 'I don't respect a man who chases after prostitutes, even when he's working.'

"I wanted to know what he meant, of course, and he told me that everybody along the block, all the doormen, knew about how Hubbard had a thing for hookers, particularly redheaded ones. I asked how he knew, and he said that sometimes the girls would hang around the building in the evening, trying to make a score with him."

Wolfe made a face. "Do these women normally infest that neighborhood?"

Fred shifted in his chair. "Not really—at least as far as I know. Their usual territory is farther south, close to the big hotels. But I think a few work their way north sometimes."

Saul sensed Fred's discomfort and cut in. "Yeah, he's right, Mr. Wolfe. The action is in midtown, but some of the streetwalkers do go up farther, particularly if they can get a regular customer. If the word got around about this character, it's possible a few might drift by to see if they could develop some business."

Wolfe scowled again. He had once described prostitution as an unimaginative vocation peopled by unhappy practitioners catering to unpleasant clients. When I asked how he knew, he glared at me and went right on talking. Whether you agree with Wolfe or not, New York has plenty of practitioners, particularly of the streetwalker variety. For anyone who spends much time outside, they seem easier to find than a taxi, and they come in all shapes, sizes, colors, and ages, including some pathetically young ones.

"I was sort of interested in the hooker angle," Fred went on, "so I asked Callaway if by chance there'd been any of them around Stevens's building the night of the murder. That made him a little suspicious; when he asked why I wanted to know, I told him I was a private cop working on another case in the neighborhood, and I said I had just wandered down this block out of curiosity to see the murder site. He seemed to buy that. He said that on Wednesday night there'd been a big party in his building, and he was so busy opening car doors and ushering people in that he didn't notice what was going on down the block. He said the first he knew something had happened was when a police car parked in front of Stevens's building later in the evening. Around eleven o'clock, he thought."

As Fred went on, Wolfe seemed to lose interest. I could always tell; his eyes traveled around the room—to the bookshelves or the clock or the globe. By the time Fred had finished, he'd already rung for beer, and I took orders from the others. Fred had beer also, and when Saul asked for cognac, I decided that sounded good for me, too.

We resettled with our drinks, and Wolfe began asking Fred about the block: the relative position of Callaway's building to the murder site, the width of the street, the size of the trees. He's grasping, I thought, trying to show us he's at work, but he really doesn't know where the hell to go. I was ready to cut in when he stretched both arms out in front of him, palms down on the desk. It's not a gesture he uses often, but the few times I'd seen it before, it preceded an order.

"Saul. Fred. You can say no to this if you want to. Indeed, I won't blame you if you do; were our positions reversed, I would almost certainly refuse the assignment myself, out of both helplessness and distaste." He inhaled and let the air back out slowly. "I want to know if a prostitute, redheaded or otherwise, called on Mr. Hubbard when he was at work Wednesday. And if so, I want her brought here." He leaned back and took a sip of beer.

"Lovin' babe," Saul said just above a whisper. "There must be five thousand of 'em in New York." He took a sip of cognac and turned to look at Fred, who was staring down into his beer glass. Then they looked at each other, and Saul turned to Wolfe. "I think we should get started right away," he said. "I've got a few ideas on how we should proceed, and I'd like to talk them over with Fred." They each took one last swallow and got up to leave. To be hospitable, I walked them to the front door and wished them luck. There was no joking this time, only handshakes.

Wolfe had just poured his second beer and was glowering at the foam when I plunked down at my desk. "Helplessness and distaste, huh? A cute little phrase, but you knew damn well that they wouldn't turn you down, even on an insane go-around like this."

"Archie, I won't argue the merits of the assignment, but I've never known Saul or Fred to be intimidated by what you call long odds, and besides, the thorough hunter can ill afford to overlook any thicket, however dense."

"So now we've gone from fishing to hunting, have we? Okay," I said with a shrug, "you're paying them, and for Saul alone, that's a hundred-and-a-half a day now, plus expenses."

Wolfe returned the shrug and opened a seed catalog. "Are the germination records current?"

That's another of his conversation-ending lines, so I pulled out the records, which were in fact not current, and began working, but only after I'd treated myself to a cognac refill.

17

It snowed all morning, so that by noon the plows were whining and scraping outside on Thirty-fifth Street. I'd slept late, and by the time I got myself together and went down to the kitchen, it was ten-fifteen. Wolfe wasn't around; on Sundays, he abandons his weekly schedule, usually staying in his room until at least noon. Fritz was ready for me with a pot of coffee, the Sunday *Times*, and sausage links and wheatcakes ready to go on the griddle. He asked how the case was coming, but I told him to try me later, maybe tomorrow. This was the fourth day since the murder, and already the *Times* had bumped Milan Stevens off the front page. They did have a long page-three story, though; it said that a spokesman in the D.A.'s office hoped that Gerald Milner's trial could begin "in the next few weeks." Further down in the story was a mention that the Stevens memorial service would be held Monday afternoon.

After polishing off six wheatcakes and five sausage

links, I refilled my coffee mug and went to the office. My desk calendar had just the single notation for Sunday: I had penciled in "three from Symph." at four P.M. Turning to the phone, I dialed Jason Remmers's number, and for the second time in as many days, he answered himself. He was only too happy to provide what I asked for: thumbnail biographies of the three who were coming to see us today. I took down his comments in shorthand and thanked him for his trouble, then did my own editing. I typed out brief summaries of each of the three, and by single-spacing was able to fit it all on one sheet, which I put in the center of the blotter on Wolfe's desk. Here's how it read:

CHARLES MEYERHOFF: Age, about fifty. Has been managing director of the Symphony for six years. Home town, Pittsburgh. At one time a violinist with orchestras in Minneapolis and Cincinnati, later had management position with Pittsburgh orchestra before joining Symphony. Known to have quick temper, resented Stevens and his power in the orchestral structure. The two argued frequently. Divorced. No children. Lives alone in the Brompton Arms residence hotel.

DAVID HIRSCH: Age, early forties. Has been associate conductor of New York Symphony for five years. A top-notch violinist, he also is an aspiring composer, but has been unable to get Symphony to play any of his works. Was hostile to Stevens because of this and also because he felt he was passed over for the conductor's job. Austrian by birth, moved to the States in his teens, Remmers thinks. Married, no children, lives in Ridgewood, New Jersey.

DONALD SOMMERS: Age, twenty-eight. Outstanding flutist, has been with Symphony three years, a soloist on numerous occasions. Juilliard graduate and native of Boston, he was a prodigy, played in concert with Boston Symphony as a teenager. Had a deteriorating relationship with Stevens, told Remmers he thought Stevens wanted to drive him out of orchestra. Single, lives on Gramercy Park.

Just as I got back to my desk, the phone rang. It was Lucinda. "Archie, I just remembered something that might be important—you know, on the subject we talked about yesterday."

"Okay, shoot," I said, poising a pencil.

"No, I'd rather not talk about it over the phone. Couldn't you come up?"

I tried to tell her the telephone lines were perfectly safe, but it was obvious she was holding out for another personal visit. I looked out at the snow and shuddered, but said I'd be along as fast as I could. Leaving a note on Wolfe's blotter next to the sheet of biographies, I pulled on overshoes and heavy coat and charged out into the mini-blizzard.

By some miracle I found a taxi within a block and was at Lucinda's ten minutes later; all sane New Yorkers were at home and the streets were deserted. This time I didn't get any of the boredom-and-snobbery routine from the lobby crew. They seemed to be expecting me, and the hallman even gave a fair impersonation of somebody trying to be friendly, which I halfheartedly returned.

Things also went more smoothly inside Lucinda's apartment than the day before. This time I didn't get a twenty-four-minute shuffle. In fact, she was waiting in the white-on-white-on-white sitting room, wearing a gauzy full-length number the color of raspberry sherbet when Miss Mouse ushered me in. "Archie, I'm glad you could come so quickly," she said from a sofa, looking up to be kissed. I aimed discreetly at her cheek, but damned if she didn't turn her face at the last instant and lay one square on my lips, with her own slightly parted.

I had to brace myself or she would have pulled me down on top of her, and for a second I came pretty close to letting her do it. But I finally broke the hold and slid, almost gracefully, onto the sofa next to her. "That was a four-star welcome," I said, smiling and running a hand through my hair. "And as much as I'd like to find out what you do for an encore, I think we'd better get to business. For starters, what was it you remembered that's so important?"

"Oh, Archie," she said, returning the smile and putting an arm across the top of the sofa behind me, "I apologize if I came on so boldly, but I told you yesterday how good-looking I think you are. I guess I just let myself . . ." She trailed it off, and in too studied a way, I thought. "Archie, after you left yesterday, I got to thinking about all the times I had been with Milan, all the things he had ever said that had any connection with the orchestra. There *was* something once, it must have been close to a year ago. It seemed so unimportant at the time . . ." She really liked using the trailing-off trick.

"Tell me about it," I said, lighting a cigarette.

"Well, as I remember it, we were right here in this room, having drinks. By the way, can I get you something?" I shook my head and she went on. "Milan was quite upset that evening. It seemed that he and Mr. Hirsch had a meeting in Milan's office at Symphony Hall to talk over some orchestra matters, routine things. I gather they would meet often to do that. Anyway, this day there was a strong argument—I can't even remember if Milan said what it was about. But Mr. Hirsch started the argument and became very agitated. Milan said that at one point he stood up, banged his fist on Milan's desk, and said something like 'I'd kill before I saw this orchestra go to hell. And if things keep on this way, that's where it will go.' I may have the words a little wrong, Archie, but that's basically what he said.

And he used the word 'kill,' although you know how people talk sometimes."

"And you don't know what the argument was about?" I asked.

"I'm not sure Milan ever said. What I remember most was how upset he got about Mr. Hirsch's temper."

"Was he afraid for his own safety? Did he say anything about that?"

"Oh no, no, he never mentioned it. Milan didn't ever seem to fear for himself. I think his main concern was for the orchestra. And he felt his associate conductor wasn't supportive of him."

"Not from the sound of it," I agreed, drawing on my cigarette. "Tell me, why didn't you tell me about this yesterday?"

Her answer was a coy smile. "You made me nervous, Archie. I guess you could say I wasn't thinking straight . . . all those questions, all the strain after what happened."

She was one hell of an actress, that was for sure. She knew where to make the pauses, which words to accent, how to tilt her head. It was almost like watching one of those British whodunit plays Lily drags me to every so often.

"While I'm here and we're on the subject, do you happen to know Donald Sommers?" I asked.

"From the orchestra?" Lucinda paused and pushed back a stray hair. "I don't really know him, but I've met him a few times."

"Did Stevens ever say anything about him, anything negative?"

"You mean he's another one who is suspected?" she asked, shifting to face me.

"I didn't say that." I grinned. "I was just curious because I've heard his name a few times."

"I think perhaps he and Milan had fought over a solo

once. But he is so young—he *looks* so young. I would think of him as just a boy."

"A boy who's pushing thirty."

She shrugged. "Well, I somehow got the feeling that Milan wasn't fond of him, that maybe he would be happier if he were not a part of the orchestra."

"You seem to be remembering all kinds of things that you couldn't yesterday," I said lightly.

"Oh, Archie, please don't tease me. I really can't recite anything specific that Milan said about Mr. Sommers. It's just an impression I got."

"Okay, one last thing before I go. How would you describe Stevens's relationship with Charles Meyerhoff?"

Another shrug. "Maybe somewhat strained. But to be honest, I don't ever remember Milan talking at all about Charles to me."

"Could that have been because you used to go out with Meyerhoff?"

"That of course is possible," she said. "But I never once got the feeling Milan felt any bitterness toward Charles for any reason, and although I haven't seen Charles that much recently, I never sensed any dislike for Milan on his part. But then"—she stretched out both arms palms up and did another eye-roll—"what do I know?"

"You know a great deal," I said, "but whether I'm hearing all of it is a different matter." When she started to protest, I held up a silencing hand and said I really had to go, but that she'd be hearing from me or Wolfe. We wrapped our arms around each other at the door, and I was the one who finally broke the clinch, or we might still be there.

It was harder getting a cab back, and it was after one when I walked into the office. Wolfe looked up from a book, his face a question mark.

"Lucinda F-M is really something," I said, slipping into my desk chair. "Seems she had a sudden burst of recollection and had to share it with me." I then gave him a verbatim report, leaving out only the details of our opening and closing embraces, which he wouldn't have appreciated anyway. "Has your opinion of her changed since yesterday?" he asked after I had finished.

"I think I trust her less than I did. Maybe it's all those damn theatrical poses she strikes," I said. "Also, she seems to have a very selective memory. If you're looking for odds on whether she did it, I'm still not ready to give any, though. Maybe that's because she kisses so well."

Wolfe grimaced and picked up the sheet with the thumbnail biographies. "They're all still coming?"

"Yes, sir, at least as far as I know. I talked to Remmers this morning—that's where I got the biographical stuff. Do you want to see them all at once, or should I hold them in the front room and bring them in one at a time?"

"All at once. The interaction may be instructive to watch, particularly if Mr. Meyerhoff does indeed have a quick temper. Has Saul or Fred called?"

I said they hadn't and he nodded, then picked up his book and submerged himself while I went back to playing catch-up with the orchid records.

If nothing else could be said for that Sunday-afternoon visit, at least they arrived promptly: My watch read two minutes past four when the doorbell rang. Through the one-way panel, I didn't have any trouble figuring out which body was attached to which name. Meyerhoff was standing in front of the others, and he didn't look happy. He was the shortest of the three, with wavy brown hair that was retreating up his forehead and probably would disappear altogether in the next ten years. The one with horn-rimmed glasses had to be Hirsch, if for no other reason than age. He was three or four inches taller than Meyerhoff and had a scraggly mustache, and his face wasn't filled with sunshine either. Sommers was a head taller than Hirsch, and even with his black topcoat on, I could see that he was nearly as thin as the instrument he played. He had shaggy black hair and eyebrows, and his own expression was one of worry rather than anger.

The bell rang for a second time just as I swung the door open. "Good afternoon, gentlemen, please come in," I said in a hearty tone. "Awful day, isn't it?" I got only grunts in reply, and my calling each by name as I helped him off with his coat didn't seem to make an impression. "Where's Wolfe?" Meyerhoff demanded. "I want to get this over with fast."

I led them to the office, still playing the hearty butler role. Before I was finished with the brief introductions, Meyerhoff had attached himself to the red leather chair and thrust his chin at Wolfe as if daring him to challenge the choice of seats.

It didn't get a rise. Wolfe acknowledged each of them with a nod, then slipped the gold strip into his book and put it down deliberately. His eyes settled on Meyerhoff, then went to Hirsch, seated next to him in a yellow chair, and finally to Sommers, who had been left with the yellow chair closest to me.

"We can give you a half-hour, no more," Meyerhoff said loudly, looking at his wrist. "We wouldn't have come at all, except that Jason asked us to. I can't see any reason for this, what with—"

"A moment, please," Wolfe said, holding up a hand. "If you'll indulge me in a preface, Mr. Meyerhoff? Thank you. I assure you my admiration for brevity is at least equal to your own. Before we begin, would anyone care for refreshments? I'm having beer."

Meyerhoff gave a vigorous shake of his head, which seemed to set the mood for the others. They also declined, although more graciously.

"Very well," Wolfe said, touching his buzzer and giving them the once-over again. "As Mr. Remmers told you and as you have no doubt read in the papers, I have been hired to identify the killer of Milan Stevens. Now, I—"

"This is crazy!" Meyerhoff roared. "Everybody knows who killed Milan. The police got the right person, and they got him fast. Why can't we just—"

"We seem to be interrupting each other, Mr. Meyerhoff," Wolfe snapped. "If you please. You've all taken the trouble to brave execrable weather to get here, and I thank you for it. You moments ago expressed your desire that this meeting be brief. It can only be so if you allow me to continue. You'll all have your turn to speak."

"God, you're every bit as arrogant as I'd heard," Meyerhoff said, crossing his arms. Then he gestured to me. "Is he going to stay in here taking notes?"

"Arrogant?" Wolfe asked, lifting his shoulders a quarter of an inch and dropping them. "Perhaps, although I prefer 'self-possessed.' As to Mr. Goodwin, yes, he is present at all meetings in this room. And his faculties are such that if he did not take notes, he could nonetheless reconstruct verbatim a conversation of several hours' duration. I had no idea anyone would object to his attendance. After all, each of you also is a witness to everything that will be said here." Wolfe focused on Meyerhoff, who scowled but didn't open his mouth.

"Now, if I may go on," Wolfe said, pouring beer, "Mr. Milner has of course been charged with murder. He is known to have been in the Stevens apartment on Wednesday night, and is also known to have had a confrontation backstage with Mr. Stevens recently, a confrontation that centered on Mr. Milner's relationship with Maria Radovich. These are well-documented occurrences, and I do not quarrel with them. For my own reasons, however, I believe someone other than Mr. Milner killed Milan Stevens."

"And what might those reasons be?" It was David

Hirsch, his Austrian origins showing in a slight accent. He cleared his throat and fidgeted.

"No, Mr. Hirsch," Wolfe said, "as I stated, they are my own reasons, and I'm not prepared to share them right now."

"This sounds like a fishing expedition to me," Meyerhoff barked. "Your reputation for exorbitant fees is well known in this town. You've got a client who doesn't want to believe the man she loves committed murder—the murder of her own uncle. Enter Nero Wolfe. She turns to you, and you accommodate by calling in anyone who ever had words with Milan. Oh, don't think we don't know why we're all here; we talked about it on the way over. Each of us has at one time or another gone at it with him—and me more than anybody, it's true. But we're not alone; there are others in the orchestra who've fought with him or have some reason to resent him. I'll be glad to supply you with names—then you can spend the next month questioning them, too." Meyerhoff, who'd been leaning forward during his little speech, slouched back into the chair and folded his arms again.

"I appreciate your offer," Wolfe said dryly. "I also appreciate the mention of your various disputes with Mr. Stevens. It saves me the trouble of having to bring it up as the *raison d'être* for this gathering." He paused for a sip of beer. "Mr. Meyerhoff, since you brought up the subject, I'll ask you first: What were the bases of your disagreements with Milan Stevens?"

"I assume you know at least a part of the answer to that question already, from your talks with Jason. But as long as I'm here, I might as well indulge you, to use your own word." He leaned forward again, elbows on the arms of his chair. "I've been managing director of the Symphony for a little over six years now. When I joined it, the orchestra was in chaos. The music director at that time was incapable of exercising authority and maintaining discipline—I think that's a fair statement, isn't it, David?"

Hirsch nodded, grim-faced. "Yes, in fact an understatement. 'Chaos' is the word I'd use, too."

Meyerhoff went on. "The Symphony board decided after several years of badgering from a number of us that a change had to be made. It was about then that Jason became chairman, and he was strongly in favor of hiring Milan, who at that time was in London. Milan had a well-known name in music circles, particularly in Europe, but from musicians and other orchestra people I'd heard things about him that I didn't like."

"What things?" Wolfe asked.

"Well, for one, his choice of repertoire. Instead of trying to introduce his audiences to some of the lesser-known composers and some more contemporary music, he invariably took a safe 'popular' tack: a lot of familiar, comfortable works—by all the favorite composers. But you'd rarely see him conduct Berg or Schönberg or Bruckner, or give the premiere of a new work. I felt the Symphony should be more innovative and experimental in its repertoire. You need some of the traditional and the popular, yes, but there should be a balance. Stevens simply was not the man to supply that balance." All the while Meyerhoff spoke, Hirsch nodded at varying speeds.

"Another thing was Milan's personality," Meyerhoff continued. "The Symphony needed discipline, yes, but not despotism. This is an orchestra of great individual talents, Mr. Wolfe. For instance, Don here is the finest flutist in the United States, perhaps the world." Sommers flushed and muttered a denial. "Yes, you are, Don, and I'd say it whether you were sitting here or not. Anyway, the Symphony is loaded with great talent, and it takes a skilled, tactful music director to make these marvelously gifted individuals play well together. You don't do that with an iron hand alone; there must be a subtle mixture of understanding and discipline. I know one shouldn't speak ill of the dead, but the truth is that Milan Stevens simply didn't have the warmth to handle the situation. He could keep order, but he lacked the humanity necessary to coax greatness from his players.

"Time and again I talked to him, urged him to loosen up and be more flexible. But the answer was always the same: 'There is no substitute for firmness, and they must know who is boss.' And whenever I suggested he modify his approach, he became angry."

"Mr. Hirsch, do you concur with this assessment?" Wolfe asked.

Hirsch cleared his throat again. "Yes, yes I do. I was also associate conductor under Milan's predecessor, and when Milan was chosen, I was disappointed. I won't deny that I'd hoped I might be picked as music director myself, but"—he shrugged in acceptance—"that was not to be. I resolved to work with the new director, but almost from the beginning, Milan made it clear to me by his actions that I would have almost nothing to say about how the orchestra was run. I often wondered why he even kept me around, but one day I figured it out. It didn't matter who the associate conductor was; under Milan Stevens, he would have very little responsibility, so he probably felt it might as well be me as anyone."

"I understand you have a composition that you hoped the orchestra would someday play," Wolfe said.

Hirsch passed a hand over his forehead. "Yes, that's so," he said after a pause.

"But it was not played?"

Another pause. "No. Milan apparently felt it was not . . . of sufficient caliber to merit a Symphony premiere." Hirsch compressed his lips.

"Why 'apparently'?" Wolfe asked.

"I say 'apparently' because Milan never came right

out and said the symphony wasn't good. But every time I brought it up, he changed the subject or put it off by saying something like 'Oh, yes, we've got to sit down and talk about this when things ease up, but right now is such a hectic time.' He was always too busy. And yet I know it is a good work—I've shown it to many people in the music world whose opinions I respect, and every one has been enthusiastic, far more than they needed to be just to make me feel good."

"Other than its quality, what reason might Mr. Stevens have for not playing your symphony?"

Hirsch shook his head. "I don't know, unless he just didn't want his assistant to get a share of the spotlight."

"Mr. Hirsch," Wolfe said, "was there an open hostility between you and Mr. Stevens?"

Hirsch fiddled with his glasses and uncrossed his legs. "I wouldn't say so. We did argue sometimes, usually in private, about his treatment of some of the orchestra members."

"You thought he was too much the martinet?"

Hirsch nodded. "Yes, he humiliated some of them during rehearsals, shouting insults, generally demeaning them. I felt it upset the whole orchestra, destroyed morale. Instead of getting them to play better, which I assume was the intent, it had the opposite effect."

"This was a frequent occurrence?"

"Yes, at practically every rehearsal. It was as if he enjoyed being so cruel."

"And you reminded him of it?" Wolfe asked.

"Quite often. But he would just brush me aside. 'They are professionals,' he would say, 'and I expect them to play like professionals, not like members of some community orchestra.'"

Wolfe shifted his weight. "Is it true, Mr. Hirsch, that you once told Mr. Stevens you would kill for the orchestra?"

"What?" Hirsch twitched like he'd just gotten a high-voltage jolt. "Who told you that? I never said such a thing!"

By this time, both Meyerhoff and Sommers were trying to jump in. "Gentlemen!" Wolfe snapped it off. It wasn't loud, but it shut all three of them up. "If you please, at the risk of being repetitious, you'll all be able to leave here sooner without interruptions." He turned back to Hirsch.

"It has been said that you spoke the following, or something very similar, at a meeting in Mr. Stevens's office: 'I'd kill before I saw this orchestra go to hell. And if things keep on this way, that's where it will go.' Well, Mr. Hirsch?" Wolfe's eyes narrowed.

Beads of perspiration were forming on Hirsch's nose bridge, above his glasses. He looked at Meyerhoff and Sommers, then licked his lips. "Mr. Wolfe, I never said that, or anything like it." His voice was tense but low, and he accented each word. "I don't talk that way," he continued, gaining speed. "Ask anyone I know. I wouldn't use a word like 'kill,' or even 'hell.' I can't—"

"That's true," Meyerhoff cut in. "I've never heard David—"

"Enough!" Wolfe spat, silencing Meyerhoff. "Mr. Hirsch, please go on."

"I started to say, I can't imagine who would make up a story like that. It just isn't true. I was angry with Milan quite a few times—many times—but I would never, ever say such a thing." He looked around again, at each one of us, and then down at his lap. I started feeling sorry for the guy.

"Mr. Hirsch," Wolfe continued, "can you imagine why anyone would concoct such a story?"

"No, I don't think I have enemies within the orchestra, other than . . ."

"Yes?"

"Other than Milan," Hirsch said, slumping in his chair.

"You considered Mr. Stevens an enemy?" Wolfe asked.

"No, but I think he considered me one," he said.

Wolfe eyed Hirsch. "Were you planning to resign?"

"I had . . . considered it at one time, but recently Charlie—Mr. Meyerhoff—had said there might be a change in music directors before too long."

Wolfe turned to Meyerhoff. The managing director leaned forward on his elbows again. "That's true. Jason had always been Stevens's big defender, and the board pretty well went along with whatever Jason wanted. I've been telling him for over a year how bad the orchestra's morale is, and recently he seemed to be coming around to my view, although he was giving up very hard."

"I gather that if Milan Stevens were to have been fired, it would have been a major setback for Mr. Remmers," Wolfe said.

"Yes, I think that's a fair statement," Meyerhoff said. "He had made a lot out of our getting Stevens originally, and it hadn't improved things at all—in fact, just the opposite."

"Did Mr. Stevens resent you?" Wolfe asked Meyerhoff.

"I'm sure he did—he resented anybody who tried to tell him what to do in any way at all."

"And did you in turn resent him?"

Meyerhoff shrugged. "I guess you might say I resented what he was doing to the orchestra, his inability to pull it together, his refusal to show them any warmth or understanding."

Wolfe drained his second beer and set down the glass. "Lucinda Forrester-Moore had been a frequent companion of Mr. Stevens's recently. Is it true that you and she once spent a lot of time together?"

Meyerhoff smiled for the first time since he'd set foot in the brownstone. "Oh, we'd gone to a number of plays and parties and dinners together—just a thing of convenience," he said gently. "It was never what you'd term a serious relationship."

Wolfe nodded and shifted his attention. "Mr. Sommers, I hadn't meant to omit you from this discussion. Will you share your feelings on your late music director?"

Sommers uncrossed and recrossed his long legs. "They're pretty much like David's and Mr. Meyerhoff's," he said in a high-pitched voice that seemed somehow to go with his build. "He was certainly anything but a warm man, at least in his dealings within the orchestra. As David said, rehearsals were grim affairs, and he often singled out musicians who he felt weren't doing as well as they should.

"I don't want to come on like I'm paranoid," Sommers said, "but I'm sure Mr. Stevens wanted to be rid of me. I could tell by the way he acted whenever we discussed anything one-on-one, such as a solo I was going to do. He always seemed terribly impatient with me. And then there was that newspaper article . . ."

"Yes?" Wolfe asked.

"A few weeks ago in a Sunday interview, Mr. Stevens said that several soloists were more interested in their own careers than in the good of the orchestra. That article ran just two weeks after one of my solos, and I'm sure he meant me specifically. Again, that sounds paranoid, doesn't it? Well, I *do* think he was out for me."

"*Are* you more interested in your career than in the orchestra as a whole?" Wolfe asked.

"I love the Symphony," Sommers said. "It'd always been my goal to play here, even when I was growing up in Boston. I would never have done anything that ran against the orchestra's best interests, and I always thought of myself as a team player."

"Would you have left the Symphony if you felt Mr. Stevens was holding you back?" Wolfe asked.

Sommers looked at both Meyerhoff and Hirsch before talking. "I haven't told anyone this, but now I suppose it doesn't matter. I'd thought a lot lately about leaving. Chicago was interested and so was Boston, and I had some initial talks with people in both places."

Meyerhoff looked stunned. "Don, why didn't you come in and at least talk to me first?"

"I know, I know, I should have," Sommers squeaked, holding up a hand. "But I had to sort this out myself. I didn't want to leave, but . . ."

"You see?" Meyerhoff said, bounding from his chair and leaning on Wolfe's desk with one arm. "You see now what that man was doing to our orchestra? Here's the finest flutist anywhere, a man who loves the Symphony, and he was being driven away."

"Please sit down, sir," Wolfe said peevishly. "Your point is made, and I prefer having people at eye level." Meyerhoff shook his head and sat down. "Thank God you'll be staying with us now, Don," he said. Sommers nodded and smiled weakly.

"Well, Mr. Sommers, it seems that congratulations are in order," Wolfe said, turning back to the flutist. "You've decided that without Milan Stevens, the New York Symphony is a better place to work, is that true? Is that a fair statement?"

"I didn't say that," Sommers croaked.

"But it seems apparent. Do you deny it?"

Sommers looked down and then back up at Wolfe. "No, but I had nothing to do with his . . . death."

"You'll have a chance to prove that," Wolfe said dryly. "We've already gone well over your half-hour, Mr. Meyerhoff," he continued, looking at the wall clock. "Because this is a murder investigation, two basic questions need of course to be asked of each of you: One, did you kill Milan Stevens, and two, where were you Wednesday evening between seven and nine o'clock? Would you like to start, Mr. Meyerhoff?"

"Of course I didn't kill him—we all know who did, although I would never have guessed Milner had it in him. As to where I was—not that it really matters—I

had a lot of desk work to grind through, so after supper I went back to my office in Symphony Hall and
worked until, oh, it must have been close to ten."

"Was anyone there with you?"

"No, I was alone. There's a night watchman, but I
didn't see him in the lobby when I left. He must have
been somewhere else in the building."

Wolfe turned to Hirsch.

"Did I kill Milan? Definitely not," he said curtly.
"And on Wednesday night, my wife was out playing
bridge. I stayed home reading and listening to music.
And to answer your other question, yes, I was alone
from about seven until, well, it was ten-thirty or so
when she got home. But I can assure you I was there
the whole time. We live in New Jersey—Ridgewood—
and I took a commuter train that got me there just
after six."

Wolfe turned to Sommers, who swallowed hard and
uncrossed his legs again. "A classmate from Juilliard
was in town from Denver," he said, "and we went to the
theater that night. I think I may still have the stub at
home if you want to see it."

Wolfe shook his head. "No, that's not necessary, but I'd
advise you to keep it. Is your friend still in New York?"

"He's gone back to Denver, but I can give you his
name and phone number if you want to—"

"Don, this is ridiculous!" Meyerhoff snapped. "This
man isn't a policeman, you don't have to explain anything to him. Let's get going—we've given him too
much time already." Meyerhoff was on his feet, and the
other two looked uncertainly at Wolfe, who made no
move to stop them. They tramped to the front hall,
with me at their heels. Meyerhoff already had his coat
on, but I was quick enough to help Hirsch and Sommers with theirs. I said good-bye, but only Sommers
replied; the others were already on their way out and
obviously not in the mood for parting pleasantries.

Wolfe was sitting behind his desk in a pout when I walked back into the office. "Jovial group, eh?" I said. "It looks like all we accomplished was eliminating Sommers, and even that isn't for sure. It's simple enough to find ticket stubs and friends who'll lie for you."

"Bah," Wolfe said, glowering at the clock. He put his hands on the chair arms and made the supreme effort to get himself erect, then headed for the kitchen, undoubtedly to monitor Fritz's progress on dinner.

18

My clock radio woke me Monday morning with the news that it was still snowing and that the seven inches that had fallen in the last twenty-four hours were a record for the date. To hell with records. When I went down for breakfast, Fritz started asking about the case again, and I told him that as far as I could see we were nowhere. "But wipe that long look off your face," I said. "At least there still *is* a case."

Fritz went right on looking glum anyway, and for that matter, I was a little on the glum side myself. After the three music men had left yesterday, Saul and Fred both called in, and neither had anything to report. "Archie, I've talked to more streetwalkers today than most traveling salesmen meet in a lifetime," Saul moaned, "and that includes a fair share of redheads. But nothing. Even after I convinced them I wasn't a cop, most of them said they never work that far north. Not enough action. I gotta go now—it's almost dark, and like werewolves, they come out at night, in case you didn't know."

I told him that's what I'd heard and gave him a keep-at-it pep talk that really wasn't necessary. I fed the same pep talk to Fred when he checked in half an hour later, only with him, it was needed. He had two reasons for his dark mood: one, he hadn't had any more luck than Saul, and two, his wife, Fanny, wasn't exactly doing handstands over the assignment. But he signed off by saying he was headed back into the streets. "Intrepid fellow," I said, hanging up.

If Wolfe was disturbed by their lack of success, he didn't show it, preferring to concentrate on the *Times* Sunday crossword. After dinner when we were back in the office with coffee, he finished the puzzle, tossed it aside with disdain as he did every week, and looked at the clock, which read eight-fifty-five. "What time is it in London?" he asked.

"Let's see, they're six—no, make that five hours ahead of us," I answered.

"Far too late to call Mr. Hitchcock," he said. "All right, we'll telephone him tomorrow after lunch." He picked up a book and began reading. I decided not to give him the satisfaction of asking why he wanted Hitchcock. Geoffrey Hitchcock is a private investigator in London whom we've used on a number of cases; we've also been able to help him a few times ourselves, which keeps things pretty well in balance. In fact, just a few months before, Hitchcock had called about an American con man who'd shifted to London and was bilking widows and divorcees. Using the *Gazette* clips and the recollections of one of Lon's best police reporters, I was able to give him a good rundown on the guy's methods, for which he was grateful. And Wolfe got a letter from him a few weeks later saying that in large part because of our help, the con man was in jail and Hitchcock collected a fat fee from an angry victim.

As soon as Wolfe got settled at his desk Monday morning following his plant-room playtime, I swiveled to face him. "Big Ben is at this very moment chiming four o'clock," I said.

He breathed deeply and scowled. "I haven't even seen the mail yet, but I suppose you'll hector me until we make the call. Confound it, yes, go ahead and get him."

Hitchcock's number was on a file card in front of me, and with the grace of New York Telephone, I had no trouble getting through. He answered on the second ring, and I nodded to Wolfe, who picked up his instrument while I stayed on the line.

"Mr. Hitchcock? This is Nero Wolfe. How are you, sir? . . . Yes, I'm in good health also, thank you. When we spoke a few months ago, I said we might ask your help again someday, and that day has come. Yes, it's a case—the murder of Milan Stevens."

Hitchcock said the London papers were filled with stories on it, and he already knew about Milner's being charged. He started asking questions, but Wolfe cut him off. "Mr. Hitchcock, I can't at this time tell you very much because I don't know a great deal myself, although Mr. Goodwin and I are certain that the killer has not yet been found. What I need from you is information on Stevens's activities in Europe before he came to America. He was a conductor in a number of places—London, of course, Milan, Munich, and . . ." He turned to me.

"Vienna," I added, and he repeated it to Hitchcock.

"My question is this: Was there an occurrence in one of these cities that could have resulted in an intense enmity toward him? I'm interested in anything you find, however trivial the incident might seem."

Hitchcock said he could check easily enough in London himself, and that he'd call a colleague in Frankfurt to find out about Stevens's years in the two Germanic cities. "I know a man in Italy who may be able to help there," he added. "I suppose you're in a hurry for this?" Wolfe said yes and Hitchcock promised to get back to us within a day. Having thus indulged me by conducting business—all of two minutes' worth—Wolfe submerged himself in reviewing the mail and filling out the order blanks from two new seed catalogs.

That afternoon, Stevens's memorial service was held at three. I thought about going, but decided I would be of more value at home in case Saul, Fred, or Hitchcock called in while Wolfe was up with the plants. None of them did, though, and about four-thirty the cabin fever was so bad that I told Fritz to cover the phone while I went for a walk. The air was cold and clear, ideal for sorting things out, I said to myself. But as I started east on Thirty-fifth Street, I couldn't find anything to sort. We were noplace, and I began to think maybe Wolfe had spent too long on the shelf, like an outfielder who holds out until May and doesn't get his batting eye back before August. Both the Saul-Fred project and the Hitchcock thing seemed like the long shots of a gambler who was way behind and trying to catch up fast. I was still muttering when I got back to the brownstone at five-thirty after having walked a good four miles. "Only one call while you were gone," Fritz said as I hung my coat up. "Miss Adjari, a little while ago. I told her Mr. Wolfe was with the plants, and she said not to disturb him, but to tell him that the services for Mr. Stevens were very nice and that she is going back to London on a plane this evening."

"Not wasting any time, is she?" I snapped, and Fritz said something about only being a message-taker. When Wolfe came down at six and settled in behind his desk, I told him about the call. The reaction was a shrug and a request to turn down the thermostat. "A damn good idea!" I said, standing up. "A little less heat might stimulate some mental activity around here—God knows we could use it. Maybe if I open a couple of windows too, we'll—"

"Archie, shut up. You're prattling. What would you have me do? Buy advertising time on television? Or erect a billboard on Times Square? Like good fishermen, we have put out our lines. And also like good fishermen, we need to exercise some patience."

"What do you know about fishing?" I snarled as I turned the heat down. "You haven't dropped a hook in the water since the invention of the reel." There was more to our conversation, but that's enough to give you the flavor, and also an indication of why there wasn't much talking at the dinner table, despite Wolfe's attempts to start a discussion on what New York would be like today if the Dutch hadn't got muscled out by the English a few centuries back. It was also quiet in the office after dinner, and when the phone rang, I almost knocked over my coffee cup reaching for the receiver.

I expected Saul's voice, or possibly Fred's, but it was Hitchcock. "Hallo, I've got a little bit for you," he said as I motioned Wolfe to pick up his instrument. "It's quite late here, you know, but I just got a call back from Frankfurt, and I knew you were anxious. First off, I should tell you that the chap from Italy was no help. Seems Stevens's years there were most uneventful. And I could find nothing here in London, either, except for some general grumblings that he was a strict taskmaster. But as to Munich," he said, "my associate in Frankfurt tells me there was one untoward incident. Happened about fifteen years ago, he can get the exact date if you like. It seems a young oboe player in the Munich orchestra named Wald, Willy Wald, was dismissed by Stevens, and rather summarily, at that. Anyway, the young man was killed in a motorcar crash less than a week later. He was alone in the car, and it went off a cliff in the Bavarian Alps for no apparent reason. The authorities ruled it an accident, but there was speculation in the press at the time about suicide. Rather nasty, as you can imagine.

"Stevens defended himself by saying that Wald hadn't been playing well enough to remain in the orchestra. The business got a good bit of publicity for a few days, but according to my Frankfurt friend, it blew over, and Stevens went on to conduct in Munich for several more seasons. I'm not sure this is of any help to you, but you said you wanted anything beyond the ordinary."

"Quite so," Wolfe said, "and I thank you for robbing from your sleep to report this. Anything else?" Hitchcock said there wasn't, and we signed off.

"Well, is that what you were expecting?" I asked.

"I don't know," Wolfe said, leaning back in his chair and lacing his fingers over his belly. He stayed that way for several minutes, then blinked his eyes and reached for his book. I started to say something, but the phone rang.

This time, it was Fred. "Archie, I've gotta go home now, or all hell will break loose with Fanny. I've had hookers laugh at me and swear at me and try to do business with me, but no luck on what we're looking for. I'm whipped."

I cupped the mouthpiece, telling Wolfe that Fred wanted to pack it in for the night, and he nodded. "Okay, make for home; maybe tomorrow will be better," I said, hanging up. "Who am I kidding?" I told Wolfe. "Tomorrow will be more of the same, and we all know it. Let me go and talk to Hubbard; if there was a hooker around the building that night, I'll find out."

"No," Wolfe said, shaking his head. "We can always do that later, if necessary. Maybe Saul will bring us news."

But Saul didn't. At eleven-twenty, he called in and said he'd talked to more than three dozen entrepreneurs of the street, without success. "But I want to keep at it, Archie. Ask Mr. Wolfe to give us some more time."

"Oh, he will," I said, watching Wolfe coax the last

few drops of beer out of his glass. "In fact, I think he may give you another month if you want it. Well, it's his money—enjoy yourself." Saul hung up, and I told Wolfe the day's excitement had been too much for me, that I was going up to bed. He looked up, nodded, and rang for more beer.

19

Tuesday was a Xerox of Monday: snow, although now just flurries; Wolfe at his desk reading and ignoring me; and Saul and Fred somewhere out there searching for a woman who might or might not exist. I clipped my nails, shined three pairs of shoes, changed the ribbon in my typewriter, and took two suits to the cleaners. Maria called just after lunch, and I told her we had several lines out. She was back staying with Lily, although she said she could face the apartment now and might move back tomorrow. I suggested she stay put for a few more days.

"The company does Lily good," I said. "Gives her somebody to spout off to about why the Democrats are God's chosen people." Maria laughed for the first time since I'd met her, and it sounded nice. I told her that if she felt up to it, I'd take her and Lily to Rusterman's that night for a quiet dinner in one of the small rooms upstairs. She said thanks, but Jerry was coming over and they just wanted to be alone and maybe would take a walk. Not to be totally spurned, I got Lily to the phone and made a date for the two of us. Lily Rowan rarely says no to a dinner invitation.

She was oozing questions about our progress, and I told her that I didn't think we were doing so hot. "But I haven't been that candid with Maria," I said, "so please don't make a liar out of me when you talk to her. We haven't got forever on this, although Wolfe's acting like it. The D.A.'s office may move slowly sometimes, but on this one they'll be trying for a fast wrap-up. I guess I would too, in their place."

At a table upstairs in Rusterman's, Lily eyed me over her wineglass. "M'love, are you absolutely convinced that Milner didn't do it?"

"Aren't you?" I asked back, doing my eyebrow trick. "You've had plenty of time to observe him the last few days. Do you think he's a killer?"

She shook her head and smiled. "I really don't, and I like to think that intuition of mine that you talk about so much really works. But who else have you got?"

"You'll have to ask my boss about that. For all I know right now, he thinks it's a suicide, that Stevens had a triple-jointed right arm and stabbed himself in the back."

That was enough business talk for the evening, and Lily knew it, so we drifted into other areas, such as who was divorcing whom in her crowd and why. That was hardly a favorite topic of mine, but Lily was so entertaining that for one stretch of at least six minutes, I didn't think once about the murder. Finally, though, she must have noticed me sneaking peeks at my watch, and for the second time in a week she suggested we should be going. "I know you're busting to be back at your desk, Escamillo. Just promise me that when you bust the case wide open—how I love that phrase—you'll let me be one of the first to know." I promised I would, and then dropped her off at her place in a taxi, arriving home myself at just after ten-thirty.

If I didn't know about Wolfe's obsession with meal schedules, I would have sworn he hadn't moved since I left. He was in the same position with the same book and the tray with two beer bottles and a glass in the same place on the desk. It even seemed like the beer in the glass was at the same level. "Anybody call?" I asked, dropping into my chair. "Saul? Fred? The mayor? The president?"

"Nobody," Wolfe said. "Was your meal good?"

I told him it was adequate, and he nodded. After Marko Vukcic's death, Wolfe had been trustee of Rusterman's for many years and had paid close attention to the cuisine and the operation. He also had made it a practice to dine there regularly, though he would have preferred being at home. Since the end of his role as trustee, he felt—and I agreed—that the quality of the food had dropped off, although for my money it was still the best spot in town for dinner if you didn't count an old brownstone on West Thirty-fifth.

"We had flounder tonight," Wolfe said, keeping his eyes on the book. "It was superb." He was getting back for my needling in the afternoon.

"Happy to hear it," I said. "They call fish brain food, don't they? Any results yet? At the rate we're moving, Milner will be doing life before we decide whether to take Saul and Fred off the job of interviewing *filles de joie*."

Wolfe set his book down and looked at me. "Where did you learn that idiom? I salute your literacy, if not your pronunciation."

"Let me translate for you," I said. "It means—"

"I'm aware of what it means," Wolfe said with a scowl. "As to the translation . . ." The sentence trailed off and he leaned back slowly in his chair, closing his eyes. I started to say something but checked myself. He sat that way without moving for quite a while, about five minutes, while I watched him, waiting.

Then it happened. At first, it was just a twitch, but soon the rhythm started. His lips began pushing out and in, out and in. I stayed still, but even if I'd said something, he wouldn't have heard it. When he's like this, no one and nothing short of a nuclear explosion can reach him. Because I've got a thing for timing, I looked at my watch when it started, then went to the liquor cabinet, poured a brandy, and settled in at my desk.

Forty-three minutes and two brandies later, Wolfe opened his eyes, taking several deep breaths. "Bah, I've been wearing blinders," he announced. "The truth has been screaming like a banshee from the housetops, but I've kept my ears plugged and my mind closed. The road has been littered with signs, and I've ignored them all. Get Saul. Get Fred. Call them off. This has been needlessly prolonged."

Perhaps by now you've figured it out too, but I hadn't. When Lily first read this, she said she realized what had happened about the same time Wolfe did, but I told her—as I have in the past—that when you're in the middle of things, the truth isn't as easy to spot as when you're paging through a manuscript. And besides, by the time Lily read this, she already knew how the story ended.

I asked Wolfe for some answers, and just as I did, the phone rang; it was Saul. "Archie, I've got her," he said. "She's right outside the phone booth and scared silly. Does Mr. Wolfe want to see her?"

"Saul," I told Wolfe, cupping the phone. "Good things seem to be coming in bunches. He says he has the lady you're looking for, and he wants to know if he should bring her over."

Wolfe nodded grimly. "Yes, Saul, come ahead," I told him. "Have you heard from Fred? . . . Well, if you happen to see him, call him in." I hung up and swiveled to Wolfe. "Okay, I think I'm beginning to get a glimmer now. Let me tell you where I am, and you can plug the holes."

For the next twenty minutes, Wolfe did fill some holes, although by then I was starting to add a few things up myself. When the doorbell rang, I went to the hall and could see that she was a redhead, all right, and not very happy. When I swung the door open, Saul introduced her simply as Mindy, and after I took both their coats, they trooped into the office.

Through the years, Wolfe has reluctantly questioned a lot of women, but this was the capper. Mindy was wearing a tight maroon sweater, beige miniskirt, and knee-high white spike-heeled boots, not to mention the long red hair that tumbled down over her shoulders. I put her in the red leather chair, and Saul took one of the yellow chairs.

"I ran into her on Fifth near Sixty-seventh," Saul told Wolfe. "She didn't seem interested in talking about anything except business at first. Then when I asked about whether she ever worked up in the Seventies, she started to walk away, swearing at me. I grabbed her, though, and told her I wasn't with the police, but that I knew a lot of them and might turn her in if she didn't help. Right, Mindy?"

She cursed and turned to me. "What's the bit, anyway? Who's the fat guy? I haven't given anybody a hassle. To hell with this." She rose to go, but Saul put a firm hand on her shoulder, and she sat back down. He looked at Wolfe and went on: "Anyway, I got her to tell me that she was up there Wednesday night. With Hubbard. I said that if she didn't talk to me, it would be worse with the police."

Wolfe considered Mindy. "Madam, I can't guarantee you protection, that's true; but it's safe to say your chances are better if you come forth voluntarily."

"But you're not a cop, right?" Mindy said, uncrossing her legs and sitting up straight in the chair.

"Correct," Wolfe said. "However, you're in a spot. We know who you are, and if we report you to the police, it will be far worse than if you admit you spent a portion of last Wednesday night with Mr. Thomas Hubbard." Wolfe was playing a weak hand; we didn't in fact have her name—none of us had seen any identification yet. But she was jumpy and knew she couldn't get out of the house easily. She licked her lips and looked at me with what she thought must have been an appealing expression, but all she got in return was a noncommittal smile.

She turned back to Wolfe and Saul again; the game was over. I poured a brandy and handed it to her, and she took a sip before Wolfe started in. This time, she opened up. Her name was Mindy Ross, from Pennsylvania, and she was twenty-three. She said she'd been in what she called her "current line of work" for eighteen months, all of it in New York. She answered each of Wolfe's questions about Wednesday night, and her description of what had happened was just as Wolfe had been telling me when Saul called.

If he was feeling smug, Wolfe didn't show it, though he had every right to be. "Archie, Miss Ross will be staying with us tonight. Show her to the South Room and explain our alarm system to her."

"Wait a damn minute," Mindy spat. "Nobody said anything about stayin' overnight. I've got to be out—"

"You don't have to be anywhere," Wolfe snapped. "You will stay at least through tomorrow. And you will probably have to make do with men's pajamas, but if you wish, some fresh clothing can be purchased for you in the morning."

I was standing next to Mindy now. She looked up at me and then at Wolfe and back at me again. She swore softly and stood, letting me direct her up the stairs to the room on the third floor behind mine where Milner had been the most recent guest. "This is the place," I said. "We weren't expecting a guest, but I think you'll find things in order. Mr. Brenner is the closest to you in size in the house, so I'll get a pair of pajamas and a robe from him. I'll also see that you get breakfast in your room, say, at eight-thirty.

"Now, as to what Mr. Wolfe mentioned: When I go to bed, I hit a switch that turns on alarms in this house. One of them is just outside your door, so that if you try to step out into the hall ..." I gestured with both hands to show the futility of such a move. "And even if you got out of your room, you wouldn't know how to open the front door—it's got a special lock. Any questions?"

She had slumped down on the bed, and was sitting there looking like she was about to cry. The hard facade was gone. "Geez, what's gonna happen? I wasn't lookin' for any trouble. I've had enough problems with the cops, I don't need this." I said something I thought would be comforting, but it didn't help, so I walked out and closed the door behind me.

Back in the office, Saul had poured himself a brandy, and he and Wolfe were talking. "Plotting for tomorrow?" I said, sliding into my chair.

"Yes, I was just telling Saul that I want everyone here tomorrow night at nine, including him and Fred. We'll also need Miss Radovich, Mr. Milner, Mrs. Forrester-Moore, and all those people from the Symphony that we've talked to, including of course Mr. Remmers. And the hallman, Mr. Hubbard. I've asked Saul to bring him here; can you arrange for the rest to be present?"

"All in a day's work." I shrugged. "I suppose you'll want Cramer, too?"

Wolfe nodded. "I'll call him myself and suggest he bring Sergeant Stebbins."

For another half-hour Wolfe sketched the plan for tomorrow. We were interrupted once, by Fred calling in to report. I told him Saul had found our woman, and that he should stop by in the morning for a fill-in on the evening's schedule. "Well, it's been nice working for Mr. Wolfe again," he said, "but Fanny's going to be awfully happy when this one's over."

"Believe me, it's almost over," I said, hanging up and turning back to Wolfe.

20

It wasn't hard following through on my assignments Wednesday morning. I started with Jason Remmers and got him at home. "Mr. Wolfe has an important announcement about the Stevens murder," I said into the phone. "He asks if you could be in his office at nine tonight, and he wonders if you could ask Misters Meyerhoff, Hirsch, and Sommers to come again, as well." Actually, Wolfe had asked *me* to get all the orchestra people, but I figured they'd take more from Remmers. He said he could make it that night, and that he'd call me back on the others. "It's extremely important that everyone be there," I stressed before we hung up.

Next was Lucinda. "You told me the other day that you always wanted to meet Nero Wolfe," I said when she answered. "Now's your chance. He thought you might like to be here at a gathering at nine tonight; it's to do with Mr. Stevens's murder."

"Oh, Archie, I already have plans," she said. "Do you

know what he's going to say?" I told her I didn't have the foggiest idea. "Well . . . if you really want me to be there, all right, I'll cancel my engagement. For you, Archie." I said Wolfe and I both appreciated it, and that we'd see her at nine.

Of course Maria gave an emphatic yes when I called her at Lily's. "You've found something out, haven't you?" she asked.

"I can't say for sure, but I do know that Mr. Wolfe wants several people to be present—including Gerald Milner." She promised to bring him along and kept pressing me for more information until I politely ended the call.

At ten, Fred stopped in to get his instructions. He was a little unhappy that Saul had been the one to locate Mindy, but it was more than offset by his relief at being able to quit what he called "the great hooker hunt."

Just after he left, Remmers called back, saying that all three from the Symphony would show up. "They don't like it much though," he said, "especially Charlie and Dave." I told him that was life and said we'd see him at nine.

Wolfe came down from the plant rooms on schedule. He rang for beer, and after a quick shuffle through the mail, asked about my progress. When I said we'd lined up everyone for the evening, he told me to dial Inspector Cramer. "With pleasure," I said, punching out the number from memory and staying on the line.

"Mr. Cramer? Good morning, this is Nero Wolfe. I wanted you to know that several people will be here at nine tonight, at which time I'll be discussing the murder of Milan Stevens. I think you will want to be present as well."

"Goddammit, I've told both you and Goodwin to butt out of this. As far as I'm concerned, the department's finished its job on the case," Cramer said.

"It's your privilege to think that, of course. But I should tell you that whether you're here or not, I plan to proceed. You can read about it in tomorrow's *Gazette*, as Mr. Cohen will undoubtedly be interested in the results."

Cramer spat a word. "Is this going to be one of your asinine charades in front of a big crowd?"

"I wouldn't choose that phrasing, but if you're asking if my office will be crowded, the answer is yes. Despite that, we'll have room for you, and for Sergeant Stebbins as well, if you care to bring him."

"I'll bring whoever I damn well feel like!" he bellowed, hanging up.

"Count on Mr. Cramer being here—with a friend," Wolfe said, leaning back and closing his eyes.

The day crawled by, maybe because I was checking my watch every two minutes or so. At four-ten, Saul called to say he'd found Tom Hubbard at home. "He was just as happy to see me as Mindy had been," Saul said. "I laid out what we knew about last Wednesday, which got him. He told me he had to work tonight, but I said that if he didn't come, the cops would probably show up later in the evening and drag him off anyway. That did it; while I was there, he called somebody to substitute, and I'm picking him up at eight."

I gave Saul a "Satisfactory" and then called Lon to tell him we'd have something late tonight for tomorrow's editions, an exclusive. He wanted it all right then, but I insisted that he'd probably have to wait until at least midnight. He said he'd be in his office all night, if necessary.

After dinner while Wolfe was sitting at his desk with coffee, I began setting up: extra ashtrays, chairs from the front room, a fully stocked bar on the small table in the corner. Fred had come at seven-thirty and was upstairs in the South Room with Mindy Ross, who'd gotten a fresh change of clothes, courtesy of a shopping trip Maria had made in the afternoon.

Saul arrived on schedule at eight-thirty with a jittery Tom Hubbard, who looked like he was going to pass out when he saw me. When he recovered, he tried to ask me what was going to happen, but I just nodded to Saul, who steered him into the front room and closed the door behind them. Now we were ready for company.

At eight-forty-three, the bell rang again. It was Inspector Cramer and Sergeant Purley Stebbins. "Ah, Inspector, you could make it after all," I said as they tramped in. "And you brought a date. It's been a while, Purley." Stebbins, who's worked with Cramer for eons and has had what he considers too many dealings with Wolfe and me in the past, nodded his long bony face but didn't smile. But then, Purley Stebbins isn't noted for his smiles, particularly when I'm around. At that, I guess you could say we've gotten along, more or less, through the years, considering our respective lines of work. He may not be the smartest man in the department, but you'll never hear me knock his courage or his loyalty. If I had to pick one guy to be on my side in a bar brawl against the Pittsburgh Steelers' defensive line, it would be Purley, although I'd never give him the satisfaction of telling him that.

"You're the first," I said, leading them to the office and explaining the seating. "Mr. Wolfe will be in shortly, and so will some others, I hope."

"Hah, he's waiting till they're all here so he can make one of his grand entries," I heard Cramer say to Stebbins as I went back to the hall. And he was right: Wolfe had gone to the kitchen at eight-fifteen, ostensibly to help Fritz with the menu planning for the next week, and said he'd be back in when everyone was seated.

They all arrived within about three minutes: first Maria and Milner, holding hands and trying to look brave; then Meyerhoff, looking just as mad as when he'd come last Sunday; then Hirsch and Sommers together, both tight-lipped and grim. Right behind them came a smiling, pipe-puffing Jason Remmers, and finally, in a white fur stole, Lucinda Forrester-Moore, who reached up and pecked my cheek as I closed the front door. "I'm the last one, aren't I, Archie?" she said with an impish giggle as we went in.

"Last is often best," I whispered, steering her to the chair nearest my desk.

Everyone else had taken the seats I'd directed them to. The front row had Maria in the red leather chair, Milner next to her, then Sommers, and of course Lucinda next to me. In the second row were Remmers, farthest from me, Meyerhoff in the middle, and Hirsch behind Lucinda. There were two more chairs against the wall, but both Cramer and Stebbins chose to stand.

I made such introductions as were necessary, including Cramer and Stebbins, then went behind Wolfe's desk and pressed the buzzer to signal him. Next I asked for drink orders. "What's this with drinks?" Meyerhoff demanded. "I certainly didn't come here to socialize. In fact, I didn't want to come at all; I'm only doing it as a favor to you, Jason," he said, turning to Remmers. "And for the second time, at that. And where the hell is Wolfe, by the way?"

"I was wondering the same thing," Hirsch piped in. "And I agree with you, Charlie. This is ridiculous. Here we are in a room with a man who's been charged with murder, and we're going to listen to another man who isn't even an officer of the law. And yet"—he turned to look at Cramer and Stebbins—"the police themselves show up and seem to tolerate this. It's absurd!"

Remmers cleared his throat. "I want to say thanks to you both, and to you too, Don, for indulging me tonight. And as long as I'm here, I'd like to order, Mr. Goodwin. Scotch on the rocks, please. Am I drinking alone?"

Sommers also had a Scotch, and Lucinda ordered brandy, but the rest passed. Just as I handed out the drinks, Wolfe appeared at the door, surveyed the scene, then strode in, detouring around the crowd to get behind his desk. He bowed slightly before easing into his chair.

"I, like Mr. Remmers, appreciate your coming tonight," he said, eyes moving from right to left and back again. "I've met you all except Mrs. Forrester-Moore. Madam." He dipped his head a quarter of an inch and she nodded, smiling. "I trust you've all been introduced, and that you've met Inspector Cramer and Sergeant Stebbins?"

"Yes, and I want to know why they're here," Meyerhoff rasped. "This gathering wasn't presented to us as official police business."

"And indeed it is not, Mr. Meyerhoff," Wolfe said. "These two gentlemen are here at my invitation and remain at my sufferance." He raised his eyebrows. "I didn't think any of you would object to their presence, though. Or am I incorrect?" His eyes swept the arc of faces again and were met with silence.

"Good, then we'll go on," he said, readjusting his bulk and ringing for beer. "One week ago tonight, as we all know, Milan Stevens was found stabbed to death in his apartment by his niece, Maria Radovich. As you also know, Mr. Goodwin had been waiting downstairs and arrived on the scene just moments later. The reason he and I knew Miss Radovich was that she had feared for the safety of her uncle and approached us for help.

"The source of her anxiety was three threatening letters her uncle had received by mail in the previous two weeks. She brought them to Mr. Goodwin and me, and they now are in the possession of the police. Miss Radovich told us her uncle had thrown these notes away and that she had retrieved them from a wastebasket. Is that correct?" he said, turning to Maria. She nodded and shifted in her chair.

"The first of the notes," Wolfe went on, "was mailed to Mr. Stevens shortly after he and Mr. Milner had quarreled in a corridor backstage at Symphony Hall, an exchange that was witnessed by several people. Not surprisingly, news of the quarrel quickly spread throughout the Symphony structure. The subject of this argument—actually it was more a diatribe by Mr. Stevens— was Maria Radovich, whom Mr. Milner hoped to marry." Milner's face and neck were red, and he kept his eyes aimed at his lap.

"Simplicity itself," Wolfe said. "The incident in the corridor, followed by the notes, and then by Mr. Milner's visit to the Stevens apartment on a night when the uncle, who was violently opposed to the marriage, was known to be home alone.

"And then the body, discovered shortly after Mr. Milner's visit. It would all seem to fit together, which is what the police and the district attorney's office even now believe. In fact, it was so neat and clean that I briefly considered Mr. Milner a suspect myself. Could he not have planned and executed this murder, intentionally having all the evidence focus on him, and then argue that only a fool would so totally incriminate himself? Possibly, but he did not make that argument at any time after the murder. And I was also quick to reject this theory because, with due respect to the officers present, the police department has not been noted for its appreciation of subtlety. One might well commit a crime and purposely make all the signs point to himself in order to be thought innocent—only to have the police arrest him anyway without looking further. And in the murder of one as well-known and esteemed as Mr. Stevens, the law-enforcement establishment would be—and was—especially anxious to make a fast arrest. If there was an obvious suspect, they would quickly seize him to still the public outcry and relieve the pressure from above.

"I was also troubled by the notes. Mr. Milner may indeed possess the cunning and courage to plan and carry out a murder, but the sending of those notes made no sense. What would he gain by such action? No, the notes were intended to make Mr. Stevens suffer additionally before his death because the intensity of the murderer's hatred for him was such that even killing was not sufficient punishment. Mr. Milner's animus toward Mr. Stevens, if indeed it may be called that, was a recent development, brought on by their conflict over Miss Radovich. Were he the murderer, his motive would not be revenge, but simply the removal of the only obstacle to his union with Miss Radovich. And the notes were patently vengeful instruments."

"Look, this is mildly interesting in an academic sort of way, but it really doesn't prove a damn thing," Meyerhoff said. "No court would give the least bit of weight to what you've just told us."

"Perhaps not, sir. This was just by way of telling you why I know Mr. Milner is not the murderer. Now I—"

"Excuse me, but I'd like to ask the inspector what he thinks of your line of reasoning," Hirsch said, twisting to face Cramer.

"I think it's so much bull," Cramer said, "but I'd also like to hear what else Wolfe's got to say, so we can all go home before sunrise. I know him better than any of you, and I can say this: Nobody's going to rush him. He'll have his say—all of it—so if you're smart, you'll keep quiet and listen."

"Thank you, Mr. Cramer," Wolfe said. "I'm an admirer of brevity, but we're dealing with a complex consecution of events, as you'll see. Now, after eliminating Mr. Milner, I looked at the other possibilities: There were a number of persons known either to actively dislike Milan Stevens or to at least have reason for being less than friendly toward him." His eyes traveled over the room again.

"Mr. Remmers, you had placed the full weight of your considerable reputation and integrity behind Mr. Stevens's appointment as the Symphony's music director, and the selection had turned out to be disastrous. It would hardly be surprising if you were to feel betrayed by your appointee. Mr. Meyerhoff, you had resented the new conductor's high-handed methods and also questioned his musical depth. And Mr. Hirsch, you were bitter, perhaps with justification, because you'd wanted the music director's job yourself, and also because your composition was ignored by Stevens. As for you, Mr. Sommers, you felt that the music director was unjustly critical of your performance and was trying to drive you from the orchestra." Sommers nodded but said nothing. "Miss Radovich, you were unhappy because your uncle was violently opposed to your choice of a mate." Maria recoiled like she'd been slapped, and started to say something, but checked herself as Wolfe went on. "Mrs. Forrester-Moore, you were frustrated because you did not receive a proposal of marriage from Mr. Stevens."

"That is simply not true!" Lucinda said, leaning forward and clenching her fists. "I know that's been said around town, but it's cruel and it's wrong. As I told Archie—Mr. Goodwin—when he came to see me, I didn't want to get married again any more than Milan did. I won't deny I was fond of him, but marriage . . . no, not at all. You can believe that or not, as you choose."

Wolfe scowled and shrugged. "In any event," he said, "I evaluated these various grounds for hostility toward Milan Stevens. Each of the affected parties may well have had just cause for at least some degree of anger or bitterness, but is any one of these reasons sufficient to fuel a murder?" He looked around the room again, stopping at each face. "I think not. No, whoever ran that letter opener into Mr. Stevens's back had to be driven by more deep-seated emotions—indeed, by an enmity far more intense than would have been generated because of his relatively innocuous acts of insensitivity and callousness."

"Do you call it innocuous when one person tries to destroy the career of another?" It was Sommers's voice.

"I'll answer one question with another, sir. Would—or did—such an action toward you cause you to commit murder?"

Sommers turned from Wolfe's gaze. "Of course not," he said.

"Now, if I may continue," Wolfe said. "Almost from the beginning, I realized that last Wednesday night's violence probably took root some time ago, perhaps long before Mr. Stevens's arrival in the United States. Had I been less sluggish and more visioned, I would have reached the truth earlier, but . . ." He raised his shoulders an eighth of an inch and dropped them.

"Before you start launching into Stevens's life history, let's get a little more basic," Cramer snapped. "How do you explain Milner and the apartment building? Nobody else went in the front way, and the back door is locked from the outside."

"If I may correct you," Wolfe said, "the hallman *says* he didn't see anyone else go in the front way. And I believe him. However, what if he was away from his post at some point during the evening?"

"Conjecture." Cramer sneered.

"No, sir, not conjecture," Wolfe retorted. "The hallman, Mr. Hubbard, was away from his desk—indeed, outside the building—for a period of perhaps ten or fifteen minutes. It was that absence that made possible the murderer's unseen entry into the building."

Everyone started talking at once, firing questions at

Wolfe and at each other. "Please!" Wolfe said over the hubbub. "If I may go on."

"You'd better back up what you're saying," Cramer said, "or I swear to God that you'll be retired permanently this time."

"I'll be the one to decide when I retire, Mr. Cramer," Wolfe said coldly. "And I'm quite capable of backing up what I say. It would be much simpler, however, without interruptions." He leaned back and closed his eyes until all the chatter had stopped.

"Mr. Thomas Hubbard, the hallman in the building where the murder occurred, has an excessive fondness for ... women of the streets, particularly redheaded ones. This is well-known along the block where he works—it's even something of a joke among his fellow doormen and hallmen, as one of my agents found out on a visit to the block.

"Milan Stevens's murderer also must have discovered this fact—it wouldn't have been hard to do—and put it to use. A prostitute with red hair was located and was paid well to stroll into the building lobby, engage Mr. Hubbard in conversation, and entice him into a car that had been parked down the block expressly for this purpose. It was while the two of them were in the car and Mr. Hubbard was distracted that the murderer entered the building. This was before Mr. Milner was scheduled to arrive and after the doorman had gone off duty for the night, so the front of the building was unguarded. The murderer took a chance on being seen by some other tenant or visitor in the lobby or the elevator, of course. If someone had indeed happened along, the project could merely have been postponed and restructured in a different format; those determined to kill can always find opportunities. Mr. Stevens would have been puzzled by the arrival of Gerald Milner, but beyond that, the evening would have been uneventful.

"But the plan went as scheduled. No one was encountered in the lobby or elevator. The murderer took the elevator to Stevens's floor and rang the bell. Stevens doubtless thought it strange that there was someone upstairs when the hallman hadn't called from the lobby first, but he opened the door to his killer—after all, it was someone he knew well. That the stab wounds were in the back is additional indication of this."

"Wait a minute," Cramer cut in again. "This thing has more holes than the Mets' infield. How did your hypothetical killer know when to go to the apartment and find Stevens home? And how did he avoid running into Milner?"

"I'll try to fill in the holes, sir, if you'll allow me. Everyone in this room probably knew of Milan Stevens's schedule, at least to a degree. His practice was to spend Wednesday nights at home alone going over the scores for upcoming performances. And it was hardly a secret that Miss Radovich had dance rehearsals every Wednesday night, too. Also, the killer knew precisely when Gerald Milner would arrive, because it was the killer who wrote to him on Stevens's own notepaper, asking that he come to the apartment at eight-fifteen."

"This is ridiculous!" Hirsch said. "If Milan was already dead when Milner got there, who told the hallman to let him come up?"

Wolfe frowned and took a sip of beer. "This will be far simpler without interruptions. The murderer wrote the note—Stevens's notepaper would be easily accessible to anyone in this room—asking that Milner go to his apartment. Then, the prostitute was contracted for, undoubtedly in advance. She lured Hubbard from the building at a prearranged time, probably about seven-forty-five, and the murderer went up unnoticed, was let into the apartment by Stevens, and killed him.

"The murderer didn't leave immediately, but rather stayed in the apartment with the corpse, waiting for

Mr. Milner's arrival. When he got there promptly at eight-fifteen, Mr. Hubbard was back at his station in the lobby: The prostitute had been given specific instructions that he must be returned to his desk by no later than five after eight. Milner asked for Stevens, Hubbard dialed the number, and the murderer picked up the phone, probably mumbling something like 'Have him come up'—just a few words, not enough for Hubbard to be suspicious of the voice.

"The murderer, who knew the building well, then moved quickly, leaving the front door ajar to allow entry for Mr. Milner and his fingerprints. The killer then left by the back door of the apartment, taking the service elevator or the back stairway down, then exiting via the rear door and the gangway that runs alongside the building. There's an iron gate to the street that's locked from the outside, but anyone on the inside can open it merely by pushing the panic bar. So the murderer disappeared into the darkness, and Mr. Milner wandered into the apartment calling Mr. Stevens's name, exactly as had been intended.

"The police have the rest of Mr. Milner's story," Wolfe said, looking at Cramer. "He discovered the body and, realizing he'd be the prime suspect, fled in alarm, leaving the apartment as he found it—except for his fingerprints—and leaving the front door open. His running away was a bonus for the real murderer, who probably thought Milner would call the police when he found the body. That he didn't made things look even worse for him than they would have.

"In any case, Mr. Milner's presence in the apartment had been definitely established. And the murderer further knew that because of the nature of Hubbard's absence from the lobby, he, Hubbard, would never volunteer that he had been gone for a few minutes. Hubbard could be expected to state—as he did—that he was on duty all evening and that Milner was the only person who had asked to see Stevens."

"Fascinating but farfetched," Cramer said. "For one thing, who's the hooker? And what does Hubbard say about all this?"

"Why don't you ask him?" Wolfe said, touching the buzzer under his desk. Everyone turned to the door, which in a few seconds was opened by Saul Panzer. Saul stepped aside and ushered an ashen-faced Tom Hubbard into the office.

"Mr. Hubbard," Wolfe said, "we haven't been introduced. My name is Nero Wolfe, and I think you've met Inspector Cramer." Before either Cramer or Hubbard could speak, Fred Durkin squeezed into the already crowded room with Mindy Ross in tow.

"Everyone is here now," Wolfe said. "Inspector, this is the young woman I was telling you about earlier. Miss Ross, do you recognize this man?" Wolfe nodded toward Hubbard.

"Yeah, that's him," she muttered sullenly, "the one I was telling you about."

"What did you tell me about him? Please repeat it."

"He's the one who . . . the car. Do I have to—"

"This is perverse!" Hirsch shouted. "Must we sit through this? What's it proving?"

"Shut up!" Cramer bellowed. "Let her go on."

"Miss Ross, how did you happen to approach this particular man?" Wolfe asked.

"I got money to go there and talk to him and, you know, take him to a car."

"Is the person who gave you that money in this room?"

"Yeah, him." She pointed at Charles Meyerhoff.

"I'm not going to stay here and take this!" Meyerhoff barked, standing up, but Purley Stebbins laid a beefy hand on his shoulder and pushed him back into his chair.

"This is a disgrace," Meyerhoff yelled, "being accused by a whore! I didn't kill Milan Stevens, and I'm not saying any more."

"Technically, that's true," Wolfe conceded, draining his glass and dabbing his lips with a handkerchief.

"What're you saying?" Cramer put in. "You heard the girl."

Wolfe held up a hand. "As I stated earlier, the truth was crying out to me, but I ignored it. First, the same phrase was used by two people at different times. 'It was just a thing of convenience,' they each said. Strange that both would use precisely the same words, unless of course they had rehearsed what they would say, anticipating questions. And why would there be questions, other than in an investigation?

"But as I said, I refused to read the sign. Then, through the efforts of an associate in Europe, I learned that Mr. Stevens some fifteen years ago had fired a young man from the Munich orchestra when he was its conductor, and a few days later the musician drove his car off a cliff, killing himself.

"The dead man's name was Willy Wald, and I ignored yet another sign until Mr. Goodwin by chance used the word 'translate' in conversation, waking me from my slumber. My German-English dictionary translates 'wald' to 'woodland' or 'forest.' Mr. Wald was the younger brother of Lucinda Forrester-Moore. Correct, madam?"

Lucinda had a trace of a smile on her face as she looked levelly at Wolfe. "I'd always wanted to meet you," she said in a low voice. "I'd heard so much about you."

"Just so. Yesterday afternoon, through friends in the press, I found that you are a German native, having immigrated to the United States in nineteen sixty-four, the year after your brother's death. You moved to New York, and a few years later married Mr. Moore, taking his name, but also maintaining an English approximation of your own surname."

"It now appears that was a mistake," she said, still smiling.

"Perhaps," Wolfe replied with a shrug, "although my ego wants to believe that I eventually would have found the answer on the duplicated phrase alone. By the way, I congratulate you on losing almost all traces of accent in thirteen years."

"Thank you," she said, dipping her head slightly.

"Also, your asking Mr. Goodwin back a second time was a tactical error," Wolfe said. "You overplayed your hand. It seemed obvious from his report of that meeting that you were trying to muddy the waters by focusing suspicion on Mr. Hirsch, and to a lesser degree Mr. Sommers—perhaps as a contingency in the event that Mr. Milner found a way to prove his innocence." Wolfe turned to Meyerhoff. "However, sir, you may be interested to know that she did not attempt to throw any suspicion upon you, despite an opening Mr. Goodwin gave her to do so.

"When I confronted Mr. Hirsch with the charge that he had made implied verbal death threats to Milan Stevens, his reaction was such that I all but eliminated him from consideration. Patently, talking in that manner was not his style."

Wolfe turned to Cramer, who had moved behind Lucinda, while Purley Stebbins remained at Meyerhoff's right shoulder. "I said that I was convinced Stevens's murder was the result of a deep-seated and intense hatred. And such hatred could indeed have been sparked by the death of a loved one—in this case, a brother.

"Lucinda Forrester left Europe shortly after her brother's death, bitter and resentful toward Milan Stevens but probably resigned to never having the opportunity for revenge. Imagine how she must have felt, years later, when she learned he was moving to the very city in which she lived. Coincidentally, she as a recent widow had been spending time with another member of the Symphony, Mr. Meyerhoff. However, she shifted her attentions to Mr. Stevens soon after his arrival here. Even then, she probably had begun to lay plans for his murder, although I doubt if she shared those plans with Mr. Meyerhoff at that time, and Mr. Stevens, who likely had never met the sister of Willy Wald in the Munich years, was totally unsuspecting. As for Mr. Meyerhoff, he grew increasingly unhappy over Milan Stevens's dictatorial ways, which steadily increased his power within the orchestra—at Meyerhoff's expense. Further, the managing director had grown deeply attached to Mrs. Forrester-Moore.

"This combination of emotions on the part of Meyerhoff was perfect for her purposes. She had for months, no doubt, been contemplating a way to avenge her brother's death, which she had always felt was directly attributable to Stevens. When the maestro and Milner had their public confrontation and word of it got back to her—possibly from Stevens himself—she had an unexpected opportunity. But as plans took form in her mind, she realized the need for an accomplice, and she approached Meyerhoff. You'll have to ask him whether he initially resisted, but in any event she was able to enlist him and they set to work.

"The notes to Stevens at home were her first step because, as I said earlier, even murder was not sufficient satisfaction for her; she wanted his suffering to be psychological as well. It turned out to be a pivotal decision, because the notes were what in effect brought Mr. Goodwin and me into the case—a case that at the time was not yet a capital one.

"Next, the pair set about studying the security in the building where Stevens lived. This was Mr. Meyerhoff's assignment, and he no doubt soon discovered that the doorman went off duty at seven in the evening, which meant that only one person, the hallman, stood between them and undetected entry. Next, Meyerhoff began inquiring about the habits of the hallman, Mr. Hubbard here. He may well have talked to the same person that Mr. Durkin did to find out that Mr. Hubbard had a certain weakness, one that would be skillfully exploited, as we have seen." Wolfe leaned back, took a monumental breath, and poured his second bottle of beer as Hubbard stood near the door, looking at the floor and fidgeting.

"It also fell to Mr. Meyerhoff to locate a woman, which he did, specifying a time when she was to call on Mr. Hubbard—a time after the doorman went off duty but safely in advance of Gerald Milner's arrival. To assure that this part of the operation went smoothly, Meyerhoff accompanied Miss Ross to the door of the apartment building and also supplied the automobile in which she and Mr. Hubbard had their *appointment.* He probably watched them from a place of concealment, making sure that Hubbard was well occupied while Mrs. Forrester-Moore entered the building.

"After she got inside, the rest was simple. She was familiar with the place, having been there many times to visit Stevens. She took the elevator up and rang the bell, and Stevens, on learning who it was, opened the door. They went back to the library, where he'd been working, and at some point when his back was turned, the former Miss Wald, doubtless wearing gloves, plunged the letter opener into his back. The first stab was enough to stagger him, and it was then easy for her, despite her size, to run the blade in a few more times to finish the job. Miss Radovich said she thought the letter opener was her uncle's, so it's possible Mrs. Forrester-Moore took it on an earlier visit to the apartment, with just such a use in mind. Anyway, after killing Stevens, she stayed in the apartment and waited for the call from the lobby announcing Milner. When it came, she probably muttered those few words I mentioned earlier, or a similar phrase. It would have been simple for her, a sometime actress, to approximate Stevens's voice for just a short sentence. After talking to the hallman on the speaker, she had ample time to flee via the back way while Milner was going up in the elevator."

Cramer started to say something to Lucinda, but she spoke first: "Mr. Wolfe, I've very stupidly underrated you. I really—"

"Lucinda, you don't have to talk to him!" Meyerhoff shouted. "He's just fishing. We don't have to stay here and subject ourselves to this slander!"

"Charles, it's done," she said. "Over. Mr. Wolfe, I started to say that despite your reputation, I didn't really think I was in jeopardy, particularly since you didn't even take the trouble to see me yourself until tonight; you sent Archie instead. Not that I minded, you understand." She turned to me with a sad smile, and for just an instant I wished Wolfe had made a mistake. "The only thing you were wrong about was my never having met Milan in Munich. I did meet him once—at my brother's funeral, but he didn't recognize me when we became acquainted here years later; my appearance had changed a good deal." Her hand went reflexively to her hair. "I was glad he didn't remember me, though, because almost from the beginning, I had made up my mind, as you said, to . . . take revenge. I'm not sorry I did it, either. But I am sorry about Mr. Milner. And I'm sorry about you, too, Charles," she said, turning to Meyerhoff, "although your dislike for Milan had grown to be almost as great as mine, I think."

Lucinda shifted to Maria Radovich. "You despise me, as you should. All I can tell you is your uncle had a side you probably never saw: He could be cold, cruel, hateful. He was that way to my brother—and to other members of the Munich orchestra, too. He killed Willy as surely as if he'd been steering the car. He humiliated him in front of the entire orchestra, called him names, derided him. You can see how he treated someone you cared for very much," she said, nodding toward Milner. She sank back into her chair and looked at Wolfe.

"Madam, since you mentioned Mr. Goodwin, I should point out that his eyes and ears are every bit the equal of my own, and in some situations, considerably better. Also, I must tell you that your little speech rings hollow, particularly your solicitude toward Miss Radovich. I, too, know that the man you call Milan Stevens had a dark side, and may indeed have been capable of driving another person to his death. Let us even assume he was the direct cause of your brother's fatal crash."

Wolfe turned a hand over. "So, powered by revenge, you plotted and carried out his murder. Should that not have been enough for you? Indeed, an argument could be made for this act of retribution in the minds of many self-respecting citizens, if not in the eyes of the law. But you had to go further, conspiring to frame an innocent person. The easy assumption would be that you did this to avoid prosecution. I think not; rather, it was your hatred for Mr. Stevens, which was so overriding that you also sought to savage the life of the person he held dearest, his niece, by destroying the man she loved. And the irony is that this man"—he gestured toward Milner—"is of virtually the same station and age as your brother was at the time of his death. Madam, hatred has become your handmaiden." Wolfe scowled and turned to Cramer.

"In case you're wondering, Inspector, you'll find that neither Mr. Meyerhoff nor Mrs. Forrester-Moore has a strong alibi for last Wednesday night. He said he was working late in his office in Symphony Hall, but claimed the guard didn't see him when he left. And she was at a dinner party that evening, or at least told Mr. Goodwin she was. But at the time of the murder, she was suppos-

MURDER IN E MINOR · 189

edly in a cab trying to find an open florist shop. However, I suppose you'll be checking all these things thoroughly."

Cramer glowered at Wolfe, but didn't say anything. There really wasn't a hell of a lot he could say. After all, for the last two hours he and Purley Stebbins had watched their work being done for them.

21

After breakfast Thursday, I walked to a news-stand on Eighth Avenue and picked up the early edition of the *Gazette*. The banner read SURPRISE IN STEVENS CASE, and there was a column of type of the previous night's events in the brownstone, plus pictures of Wolfe and me. I made a mental note to thank Lon for using the newer mug shots that I'd sent him.

It had been well after midnight when things settled down at home and I finally got around to calling him. He'd griped about the hour, but he had his exclusive, and the timing was perfect for the *Gazette*, an evening paper. Now the A.M.'s would be scrambling to catch up, but they were dead until their first editions for Friday hit the streets late Thursday night.

I got back to the house and laid the paper on Wolfe's desk blotter along with his mail just as the elevator came down from the plant rooms. "Good morning, Archie, nice to see the sun today, isn't it?" he said, positioning himself in his custom-made chair. I let him go through the mail and have a look at the paper before I turned to face him.

"By the time we got everybody out of here last night and I got through filling in Lon on the phone, it was too damn late to ask any questions, but I've got a few," I said.

"Oh?" Wolfe raised his eyebrows.

"Yeah. For instance, why weren't you suspicious about Alexandra Adjari? You didn't seem concerned when she went back to London right in the middle of this mess, but how did you know she hadn't come to New York earlier than she had said? She could have been here for several days before she came to see us, which would have made her a suspect."

"That point occurred to me as well, and one morning I called Mr. Cohen from the plant rooms. Through his connections with the customs people, he determined that Miss Adjari did indeed arrive in New York on the day she came to see us."

"Sneaking around behind my back again," I said. "Speaking of Lon, I suppose he's the 'contacts in the press' that you mentioned last night when you talked about Lucinda's past?"

"Yes, another call to Mr. Cohen when you were out. Through the *Gazette* files and European correspondents, he confirmed what I suspected: that Lucinda Forrester-Moore was indeed a German émigré, and that her name had been Wald."

"But you didn't know that Willy was her brother?"

"No, I couldn't establish that fact definitely, but it seemed almost a certainty. I felt confident in confronting her with it."

I grinned. "There were several things about last night that I liked, but the one that tickled me most was the expression on Cramer's face when he realized there were two of them in on it. I also noticed that you overcame your bashfulness about drinking a certain brand of beer in the presence of the heir. Which leads me to my last question: What would you have done if Remmers had been the murderer?"

The corners of Wolfe's mouth went up slightly, deepening the folds in his cheeks. For him, that's a smile. "I knew you would ask eventually, Archie. It's a measure of your thoroughness." He opened his center desk drawer, reached in, and pulled out four bottle caps, which he spread on his blotter.

I picked one up, then another. "When?" I asked.

"Fritz went out for them the afternoon you were at the bank getting Mr. Milner's bail money."

"Did any measure up?"

"Passable, all of them, and far superior to that unspeakable 'Billy Beer' you saw fit to present to me last summer. I'm pleased that Mr. Remmers was not one of the guilty. Any change would have been a step toward mediocrity, and as Isaac D'Israeli wrote, 'It is a wretched taste to be gratified with mediocrity.' I fervently hope my taste will never become so wretched as to be satisfied with one of these."

With that, he dumped the bottle caps into his wastebasket and rang for beer.

22

The phone was out of control all that morning, with newspapers wanting quotes and TV stations begging to bring cameras and crews into the brownstone. I fielded them all, giving the papers a crumb here and there but leaving the electronics guys out in the cold. The most interesting call came just after Wolfe had come down from the plant rooms.

"Archie, we're putting together the second-day stuff on the Stevens case, along with a sidebar piece on you and Wolfe," Lon Cohen said. "And yeah, yeah, we'll use those updated photos of both of you again. But what I want is a quote on whether Wolfe is getting back into the detecting business again."

"That's one you'll have to ask him yourself," I said. Cupping the mouthpiece, I spun to face Wolfe. "It's Lon; he has a question for you, one I can't answer."

He pursed his lips, nodded, and picked up the receiver, while I stayed on the line. "Good morning, Mr. Cohen. What can I do for you?"

"Good morning, sir. First off, congratulations on the case. And we really appreciate the exclusive."

"Thank you. You were a help to us as well, and as I've said, I like to keep our mutual-assistance relationship in balance."

"Yes, well, I hope what I'm going to ask won't throw it off too much. The *Gazette* would like to know—for attribution—if you're going back into active practice again."

"I'm not sure how you would define active practice," Wolfe said. "I've always viewed investigative work as an integral part of my existence. And at the present time I have no plans to terminate my existence."

There was silence on Lon's end. "I take it this means you're returning to work?" he finally said.

"Mr. Cohen, I see no need to elaborate. Again, I thank you for your recent aid. I must leave for another appointment now. Good day, sir."

Wolfe and I cradled our receivers in unison and I looked at him with what was probably a smirk, but said nothing.

"I seem to remember that you're somewhat behind on the germination records, Archie," he said. "I would hope that by day's end they will be current."

I could have given him any one of several answers, but I chose instead to go to the kitchen for a glass of milk. Besides, I was about to break out laughing, and I didn't want to do it in front of the big ham.

23

It all tied up nicely. As you undoubtedly know unless you were in Fiji at the time, Meyerhoff and Lucinda got life terms in a short, unspectacular trial. What you may not know if you don't live in New York or read the *Times* is that Maria Radovich and Gerald Milner were married about a month later in a chapel at St. Patrick's. Both Wolfe and I got invitations, and I went. Maria looked stunning, and Milner had tears in his eyes. David Hirsch served a few months as interim music director of the Symphony until a replacement was found, and his composition finally had its premiere, getting what the gossip columnists would call "generally favorable reviews." Last I heard, he was living some-place in New England and I guess doing well with his composing, although I don't keep up with that kind of thing. Both Milner and Sommers are still with the Symphony. The day after Wolfe broke the case, Remmers met with each of them and told them the Symphony valued their talents and wanted them to stay.

We heard this from Remmers when he stopped by to thank Wolfe again. He also tried one more time to write a check as a further expression of his gratitude. I was all for it, but Wolfe said no. "Mr. Remmers, I appreciate the gesture, but as I told you before, I was in effect paying a debt incurred many years ago. I am only now free of that debt." Remmers persisted, however, and Wolfe finally came up with a solution that allowed him to leave the brownstone smiling.

Wolfe did a bit of smiling himself a few days later. A small peach-colored envelope came addressed in a sweeping script to "Nero Wolfe, Esq." and plastered with stamps that had the Queen's profile on them. I open Wolfe's mail as a matter of practice, but I knew this was one piece he'd want to slit himself, so I left it intact on his blotter with the rest of the day's delivery. I was at my desk typing when he opened the envelope, read the letter, and read it again. He finally set it down gingerly and formed his lips in a circle. I kept typing, but I could hear the air passing in and out of his mouth. It's his version of whistling, something I had heard him do maybe five times through the years.

Fortunately, I was spared most of this performance because the front doorbell rang, and Fritz was out shopping. The guy at the door was a burly character who introduced himself as Lou. He needed a shave and had a tooth missing where it showed, but I welcomed him warmly. I told him to take his delivery down the outside front stairs to the basement, and that I'd let him in that door. After all, it was the first of fifty-two weekly calls he'd be making, and I wanted to make him feel welcome. It's not easy pushing a hand truck with four cases of Remmers on it.

ABOUT THE AUTHOR

ROBERT GOLDSBOROUGH is a long-time Nero Wolfe fan and recognized expert. Formerly an editor with the *Chicago Tribune*, he is currently executive editor of *Advertising Age*. He is author of the forthcoming book, DEATH ON DEADLINE, and is currently hard at work on another Rex Stout mystery. Robert Goldsborough lives in Wheaton, Illinois.

Share in a publishing event!
Rex Stout's Nero Wolfe returns in

Death on Deadline
by Robert Goldsborough

Here are special advance preview chapters from
DEATH ON DEADLINE, which will be available
as a Bantam paperback in August 1988, at your
local bookseller.

1

I've done my share of grousing over the years about Nero Wolfe's obsession with routine: his insistence on lunch promptly at one-fifteen and dinner at seven-fifteen, not to mention the sacred hours of nine to eleven in the mornings and four to six in the afternoons in the plant rooms up on the roof playing with his orchids. Almost nothing will get him to vary that schedule, although one day a few years back, when I was needling him about it, he put down his book, glowered at me, and sucked in a bushel of air, letting it out slowly.

"All right, Archie," he said. "Today is Thursday; I will show my flexibility by forgoing my appointment in the plant rooms if in turn you will call Saul and inform him you are unable to play poker tonight."

He had me, of course, and I backed off. For more years than I'm going to admit to here, I have played in a poker game every Thursday night at Saul Panzer's apartment on East Thirty-eighth near Lexington with Saul, Lon Cohen, Fred Durkin, and one or two others—the cast varies. I think I've missed one in the last five years, and that was because of a virus that knocked me so low that Lily Rowan, so she said later, was going to send over a priest to administer last rites.

Saul Panzer, in case you're new to these precincts, is a free-lance operative Wolfe uses frequently, but just saying that doesn't do him justice. Saul isn't much to look at, what with the stooped shoulders and the permanently wrinkled suits and the usually unshaven face that's about two-thirds nose. But don't be fooled by that or by his size, which makes him look like an aging and only slightly overweight jockey. When you buy Saul Panzer's time—and he doesn't come cheap— you're buying the best eyes and legs in Manhattan and probably in the country. He could tail a cheetah from the Battery to the Bronx during the evening rush hour without losing sight of it, or he could worm his way into the vault at that bank down in Atlanta and get back out again with the secret formula for Coca-Cola. And I mean the old—make that *classic*—formula.

You're probably wondering why I'm going on about

Saul and his Thursday-night poker game. I could say it's because this is one of the best parts of my week, which is true, although the real reason is that this story had its beginnings there. But I'm getting ahead of myself.

It was a Thursday in early May, one of New York's first bona fide spring days. Five of us sat around the big table in Saul's dining room. On my left was Lon Cohen, who has an office next door to the publisher of the *Gazette* and doesn't have a title I'm aware of, but who knows more about what makes New York tick than the city council and the police department combined. Next to him was Fred Durkin, thick and balding and a little slow, but A-one when it comes to toughness and loyalty, another free-lance operative Wolfe has used regularly through the years. On Fred's left was Saul, and between Saul and me was Bill Gore, yet another free-lance we use on occasions.

The game had been going for about an hour and a half. As usual, Saul had the biggest stack of chips, and I was up a little, with Fred and Bill more or less even. Lon, consistently the best player after Saul, hadn't won a hand, and it was easy to see why. He'd folded at least three times with what I'm sure were the winning hands, and once he stayed in the game with a pair of jacks against Fred's obvious straight. He was off his game and playing badly, and when we cashed in a little after midnight he was the only loser. "Tough night, Lon," Fred said as he slipped his profits into his wallet and left humming. For him, it was probably the first winning night in months.

Because Nero Wolfe's brownstone on West Thirty-fifth over near the Hudson is more or less on the way home for Lon, we usually share a cab after poker. "Not your night," I told him, after we'd flagged a cab on Lexington. "Seemed like you were a million miles away."

"Oh, hell," Lon said, leaning back against the seat and rubbing his palms over his eyes. "I've had a lot on my mind the last few days. I guess it shows."

"Care to talk about it?"

Lon sighed and passed a hand over his dark, slicked-back hair. "Archie, things are up for grabs at the *Gazette*. Nothing has gotten out about this yet, so what I'm telling you is confidential." He lowered his voice to almost a whisper, even though a plastic panel separated us from the cabbie. "It looks like Ian MacLaren may get control of the paper."

"The Scotsman?"

"The same, damn his sleazy, scandal-mongering hide."

"But how? I thought the *Gazette* was family-owned."

"It is, basically. Various Haverhills control most of the stock. But the way this bastard from Edinburgh is throwing dollars around, some of them are getting ready to take the money and run. The weasel's always wanted a New York paper, and now he's just about got himself one."

"How can he be so close to a deal without any publicity? There hasn't been a thing in the papers or on TV, unless I missed it."

Lon was so upset he ignored a very flashy hooker who yelled to us when we stopped for a light on Fifth. "Everybody on both sides seems to be keeping quiet, really quiet. And that even includes the ones who don't want to sell. MacLaren apparently does most of his wheeling and dealing long-distance, from London or Scotland or Canada or wherever he happens to be at the time. I don't think he's even set foot in the *Gazette* building yet. But the day he comes in as owner is the day I walk out, Archie. For good."

"You've got to be kidding. That paper's your whole life."

"Nothing's ever your whole life, Archie," he said, leaning forward as the cab pulled up in front of the brownstone. "If I was lucky to end up in heaven and MacLaren bought it, I'd request an immediate transfer downstairs. If he gets hold of the *Gazette,* it won't be the same place it is now, nowhere near. And it sure won't be a place where I'd want to work. I almost feel like I'm done there already, and so do some others who know what's going on. What the hell, my profit-sharing and pension will take care of my wife and me just fine for the rest of our lives."

Since I couldn't come up with anything intelligent to say to that, I just left it at good night, handed Lon my share of the meter, and climbed out. As the cab pulled away, I saw him leaning back again, eyes closed and hands laced behind his head.

2

The next morning, I was at my desk in the office typing a letter from Wolfe to a Phalaenopsis grower in Illinois when he came down from the plant rooms at eleven. "Good morning, Archie," he said, going around behind his desk and lowering himself into the only chair in New York constructed to properly support his seventh of a ton. "How did the poker game go last night?" It was his standard Friday-morning question.

"Not bad," I said, swiveling to face him. "I came out a few bills on the sunny side. It was a grim night for Lon, though. He's really knocked out by what's going on at the *Gazette*."

"Oh?" Wolfe said, without looking up as he riffled through the mail, which as usual I had stacked neatly on his blotter.

"Yeah. Seems the paper is about to be sold. To Ian MacLaren."

Wolfe looked up and raised his eyebrows. Now he was interested. "I've seen no report of this in the *Gazette* or anywhere else."

"I said the same thing when Lon told me about it last night. He says negotiations have been kept hush-hush by both sides."

Wolfe scowled. "I sympathize with Mr. Cohen. Without doubt, he would find it difficult, probably intolerable, to work for a newspaper owned by that miscreant."

"That's about what he said last night. I told him I couldn't believe he'd walk away after all these years, but he seems pretty well resolved to do just that."

"Archie, what do you know about Ian MacLaren?" Wolfe's expression surprised me. It's the one he usually puts on when he's about to take a case—call it a pout of resignation, accompanied by a sigh that would register on the Richter Scale. But of course we didn't have a case, let alone a client.

"Not a lot," I answered. "He's Scotch. Has newspapers in a bunch of cities around the world. London's one, although don't ask me where else. And I think maybe he's in two or three U.S. towns, too. Lon calls him a sleazy scandalmonger."

"He puts it well," Wolfe said, ringing for beer. "Mr. MacLaren is an opportunist who indulges in sensationalist and irresponsible journalism and runs his papers solely for profit."

Wolfe paused as Fritz Brenner, whom you'll hear more about later, walked in carrying a tray with two chilled bottles of beer and a glass. This occurrence, which takes place up to six times a day, is as much a part of Wolfe's routine as the plant room visits. After Fritz left, Wolfe opened one beer, poured, and flipped the bottle cap into his center desk drawer. About once a week he takes them out and counts them to see if he's gone over his limit, although I've never figured out what that limit is.

"Ever seen any of MacLaren's papers?" I asked.

"No, I only know him by reputation and by what I have read," Wolfe said, dabbing his lips with a handkerchief. "But the point you're trying to make is well taken. Is there a place nearby that sells out-of-town and foreign papers?"

"Just a few blocks from here," I said. It still amazes me, even after all the years of living under the same roof with him, that someone whose head is crammed with so much knowledge of history, philosophy, anthropology, food, orchids, and most of the other subjects in the *Encyclopædia Britannica* can be so ignorant about the city he lives in. But then, Nero Wolfe hates to leave the brownstone as much as he detests deviating from his daily schedule. For him, getting into a car, even with me at the wheel, is an act of downright recklessness. And when on rare occasions he is forced to venture forth into deepest Manhattan or beyond, he balances his fundament on the edge of the back seat of the Heron sedan he owns and grips the strap as if it were a parachute.

This is not to suggest that he was planning to go out now. No, I was to be the intrepid adventurer. "Find out from Mr. Cohen the names of newspapers owned by Ian MacLaren," he said as he finished the first bottle of beer and stared pensively at doomed number two. "I would like to see as many as are available."

"Quite a change of pace in your reading habits."

Wolfe grunted. "Maybe I'll be pleasantly surprised, although I doubt it. Also, when you talk to Mr. Cohen, invite him to join us for dinner tonight. If the notice is too short, perhaps he can come tomorrow. Or early next week."

When Wolfe invites Lon Cohen to dinner, it's usually because he wants information. Lon knows this, of course, but doesn't mind because through the years he's gotten as good from us as he's given in the form of scoops involving Wolfe's cases. Also, Lon fully appreciates Fritz Brenner's genius as a chef, not to mention the Remisier brandy that gets hauled out whenever he sits at our table.

But why Wolfe wanted to see him puzzled me. This time we weren't working on anything big, unless you count the business with Gershmann—not his real name—a wholesale diamond merchant who had an exceedingly sticky-fingered employee. But Wolfe, with some not-so-incidental help from Saul and me, had already pieced that one together and had delegated me to meet with Gershmann the next day to tell him who on his payroll had deep pockets.

So why was Lon getting an invite? I figured it must have something to do with MacLaren, since Wolfe wanted to look at some of the bozo's newspapers. But I was damned if I was going to ask him. Besides, he was now hiding behind a book, *The Good War* by Studs Terkel, so I swung back to my typewriter and the letter to the Illinois phalaenopsis grower.

After finished it, I dialed Lon's number. "Feeling any better this morning?" I asked when he answered.

"So-so. I'm just trying to get through one day at a time," he replied. His voice lacked his usual *jou de nure*.

"Glad you're so peppy. Anyway, I have two items of business. First, Mr. Wolfe wants to know if you can make it for dinner tonight—or if not, tomorrow."

"Best offer I've had in weeks," Lon said, perking up. "Tonight would be fine. What's the occasion?"

"Beats me. But don't look cross-eyed at a gift horse. Before I ask you the second question, I have to confess that I told the man who signs my paychecks about a certain Scottish party and his interest in the *Gazette*. I felt he could be trusted." I watched Wolfe for a reaction. There was no movement from behind the book.

"No big thing," Lon said sourly. "The whole town will know all about this soon enough. The other question?"

"Can you give me a list of newspapers MacLaren owns— both U.S. and foreign? Mr. Wolfe wishes to peruse a few."

"I'll be damned," Lon clucked. "I don't know why he'd waste his time, but that's his problem—or maybe it's yours. Anyway, sure, I can name a bunch of the rags for you. Just make sure he takes something for his digestion first."

Lon ticked off the titles of papers in England, Scotland, Canada, Australia, and New Zealand, plus one each in Detroit, Denver, and L.A. I thanked him and said we looked forward to seeing him.

"Okay, I've got the list of MacLaren's papers," I said to the cover of the book that was between me and Wolfe. "I'm off on a safari to hunt them down. Lon says you should be prepared for a grim experience. Are you up to it?"

I got no answer, nor did I expect one, so I went to the kitchen, where Fritz was preparing salmon mousse and a mushroom-and-celery omelet for lunch. I told him I'd be back in plenty of time to eat, then walked east to Seventh Avenue in the late-morning sunshine and headed north to Forty-second Street just east of Times Square, where the newsstand is. They had copies of two of MacLaren's American dailies; the Los Angeles *Globe-American* and the Detroit *Star*, and they also carried his London *Herald* and Toronto *Banner*. The guy behind the counter said he could special-order the others, but I figured what I had would give Wolfe all he could stomach.

Except for Toronto, they were tabloids, and their front pages made the *Daily News* and even the *Post* look tame. I won't bore you with details, but here are a few samples: The headline on the L.A. paper, which swallowed most of the front sheet, was "KILLER RAPIST SPOTTED IN LONG BEACH, COPS SAY." The only other thing on the page was a diagonal red stripe in the upper-right-hand corner with the words "WINNING SWEEPSTAKES NUMBERS —P.5!" The Detroit front page screeched in two-inch capitals: "DO SOVIETS PLAN SECRET AFGAN NUKE ATTACK?" and under the headline was a photograph of an incredibly buxom blonde in a sweater with a caption revealing that she had courageously run out on the field during a game at Tiger Stadium to kiss the first baseman. And the headline on the London paper, which blanketed page one, read "LET'S TOSS MAGGIE OUT, 10 LABOR MP'S SHOUT!"

It was a little before one when I got home. Wolfe was still parked at his desk, with the book in front of his face. He probably hadn't moved since I'd left, except to ring for beer.

"Home is the hunter," I announced, dropping five pounds of newsprint on his blotter in a stack, with Detroit on top, figuring the overendowed blonde would be a nice way to introduce him to MacLaren-style journalism.

He set his book down and glowered at the papers without touching them. "After lunch," he said, and I had to agree. Anyone with a proper appreciation for food knows enough to avoid unpleasantness just before a meal.

3

There is a rule in the brownstone that business is not to be discussed during meals. I was interested that day, as we consumed the salmon mousse and then the omelet, as to whether Wolfe would consider Ian MacLaren some form of business, or simply a topic of curiosity. Twice I brought up his name, and each time I got the answer clearly—McLaren fell into the business category; Wolfe refused to talk about him, preferring instead to hold forth on contemporary architecture, in particular the trend away from the "less-is-more" school, in favor of more ornamentation on buildings. He clearly favored the latter.

After we made the omelet disappear and went to the office for coffee, Wolfe started in on the stack on his blotter. I watched his face as he paged each of the four; it was a series of grimaces, pursed lips, slight shakes of the head, and in one case, an outright shudder. "More wretched than I had imagined," he pronounced, ringing for beer. When Fritz came in with the tray, Wolfe thrust the papers at him. "Take these and destroy them immediately," he barked.

"I wish you wouldn't hold things in," I said. "Say what you feel."

"Pfui. I assume you looked at them?"

"Yeah, I skimmed a couple as I walked back from the newsstand. Pretty grim."

" 'Grim' hardly covers it. They are abysmal caricatures of journalism. The depth of news coverage is farcical, the editorials simplistic and Neanderthal, the graphics grotesque." He thumped the stack with his finger, an unusual show of energy.

"At a quick glance, I thought the L.A. paper's sports section was pretty good," I ventured. "Lots of statistics."

"Fodder for the gamblers, no doubt," Wolfe grumbled.

"It's so cheerful here that I'd like nothing more than to while away the afternoon talking about Ian MacLaren's contributions to the Fourth Estate, but as you may recall, I have a three-thirty appointment with our client the diamond merchant. That should result in a fat check, made out to you, so it would be nice if I showed up on time."

"I have noted your unswerving devotion to duty," Wolfe

said, "and I hope you will manage to be home on time for Mr. Cohen's arrival." I had an answer ready, but before I could unload it, he was back behind his book.

I got back to Thirty-fifth Street a few minutes after five, which meant Wolfe was still up playing with his phalaenopsis. I unlocked the safe and tucked our latest check in, then wandered out to the kitchen, where Fritz was in high gear for dinner, and poured myself a glass of milk. "What's the program?" I asked.

"Breast of chicken in cream with foie gras on noodles," he said. "I remember how much Mr. Cohen liked the chicken breast another time when he was here."

"Nice choice," I said, and meant it. Fritz is a magician with chicken. But then, he also is a magician with beef, lamb, pork, veal, and any fish you can name. If there's a Cooperstown for chefs somewhere, he ought to have a spot there, with his puss and his name in capital letters on a brass plaque along with the words "He keeps Nero Wolfe happy—which alone is reason enough to be in the Hall of Fame."

My stomach already was pondering the chicken breast as I went back to the office and typed a letter to an orchid grower in Pennsylvania who wanted a peek at the plant rooms on a trip he was making to New York next month. Permission granted. Wolfe almost never denies a serious request to see his precious phalaenopsis. I call it vanity; he says it's the sharing of information, although visitors always learn far more than they could ever teach either Wolfe or Theodore.

After finishing the letter and putting it on Wolfe's blotter for his signature, I started in on the germination records but was interrupted by the phone.

"Archie, it's Lon. I'll be hung up at the office for a while yet. I'll tell you why when I get there. It'll probably be pushing seven."

I told him not to worry, that we might even postpone the start of dinner by as much as three minutes if he was late. As I turned again to the germination cards that Theodore brings down daily, I heard the whine of the elevator. My watch said six-oh-two, which meant Wolfe was on his way down from the plant rooms.

"Lon called—he'll be a little late. Trouble of some kind at the paper," I said as Wolfe came in and headed for his desk. "I'll lay nine to five it has something to do with MacLaren."

"Very likely," Wolfe said, reaching for the Torkel. "We can delay dinner if necessary." His tone told me he found the idea extremely distasteful. But he also felt—he's said so many times—that "a guest is a jewel, resting on a cushion of hospitality."

As it turned out, we were able to stay on schedule. Lon rang the doorbell at six-fifty-seven, which meant he had plenty of time for Scotch on the rocks in the office while I worked on bourbon and Wolfe downed his second beer.

"Sorry I'm late," Lon told Wolfe, settling into the red leather chair with his drink. He looked beat. "Things are jumping at our place. Turns out the *Times* is breaking a story in tomorrow's editions that MacLaren has made a bid for the *Gazette*. I don't know how they caught wind of it, but they called our chairman, Harriet Haverhill, and asked her to respond to MacLaren's statement that he was making an offer for *Gazette* stock. She gave them a 'no comment,' then called the city desk to alert them, and we really had to scramble to get something into tonight's Final."

"Indeed?" Wolfe said. "Mr. Cohen, with your sufferance, I would like to defer the subject of Ian MacLaren until after dinner. I assure you I'm most interested in hearing about him, but—"

"Say no more," Lon cut in, laughing and holding up a hand. "I agree completely. I've been looking forward to this meal, and the best way to enjoy it is with conversation on more pleasant topics."

So twice in one day MacLaren got scrubbed as a mealtime subject. And knowing how both Wolfe and Lon felt about him, I was beginning to be anxious to meet the guy to see whether he had horns, fangs, or maybe a third eye in the middle of his forehead.

Still, events at the *Gazette* hadn't noticeably damaged Lon's appetite. He managed three helpings of the chicken and went for seconds on the tart. As we ate, Wolfe held forth on why he thought the constitutional amendment limiting a President to two terms should be repealed, while Lon—bless his heart—took the opposite view. I scored Wolfe the winner, but just barely.

We left the table strewn with polished plates for Fritz to clear and crossed the hall to the office. Lon settled back in the red leather chair, with a snifter of the long-awaited Remisier at his elbow. It looked so good I treated myself to some, too, instead of Scotch. Wolfe, of course, had beer.

"Mr. Cohen, you know from Archie that I've become very curious about Ian MacLaren," he began, switching to business.

"So I gathered when he phoned and said you wanted to see some of his papers. Naturally I'm curious as to why you're curious. By the way, did you read any of the rags?"

"Enough to confirm my opinion of the man's journalistic standards. I have several questions about him, sir, but you proceed, please. You said earlier that his bid for the *Gazette* is now public knowledge?"

"Well, not quite yet," Lon replied, looking at his watch. "We learned that the *Times* will break a piece in tomorrow's editions, so our management finally got up off their collective duffs and decided to run something, if just to keep from getting scooped on our own story. But it'll only make the Late City Edition, which is less than ten percent of our circulation. It will be on the street in about half an hour."

"How serious is MacLaren's bid?"

"Damn serious," Lon said. "The *Gazette* is very closely held. Private ownership. And that ownership is in the hands of a small number of people, most of them members of the Haverhill family. All MacLaren has to do is win a few of them over."

"I want to get to the family later," Wolfe said. "First, what is your own opinion of Mr. MacLaren?"

Lon savored the Remisier. He might have been too beat to notice all this curiosity on Wolfe's part was out of the ordinary, but I wasn't. Something unusual was afoot, so I paid close attention. "As far as I'm concerned, MacLaren is the worse thing that's happened to journalism since Hearst. You've seen his papers. He's in the business for the cash. Rather, I should say the cash and the power."

"Has he ever started a newspaper?"

"Nope, in every case he grabbed an existing one by throwing money around. He's made a profit on just about all of them, so you can't knock his business success. But what he does when he gets a paper . . ." Lon scowled. "He gives it his stamp—if you want to call it that. He usuallay turns them into tabloids, fills the front page with shrill headlines, slices stories in half, throws in girlie pictures, and cuts loose with an editorial policy that's about twenty degrees to the right of Jesse Helms. As far as I'm concerned, he combines the worst of the original William Randolph Hearst and Rupert Murdoch.''

"And the owners of the *Gazette* are prepared to sell?''

"That's a question,'' Lon said, turning to salute me for keeping the Remisier flowing. "A few apparently are, from the talk I hear around the building, but whether or not MacLaren can finagle a majority of the stock remains to be seen.''

"How many owners does the *Gazette* have?'' Wolfe demanded. "And how hard would it be for this man to buy them out?''

"Okay, here's the picture. First, there's Harriet Haverhill, whom I mentioned. She's chairman of the board, the widow of Wilkins Haverhill, who bought it back in the thirties. It wasn't much then—sort of a pseudo-pulist tabloid with pretensions to compete with the *Times* and the *Herald Trib*. Haverhill made it into a broadsheet, beefed up the metropolitan coverage, and built a strong home-delivery network. And his editorials got tough with city government—so much so that La Guardia nicknamed him 'the Bulldog,' not to mention a few other unprintable names. All in all, he built the *Gazette* into a first-rate paper. He died in the early sixties, and she's been in charge ever since. One hell of a woman. She's over seventy now, and is the largest single stockholder, with a little more than one-third of all the shares.''

"Is she likely to sell?''

"Definitely not, and that's one of the most encouraging things right now,'' Lon answered. "From the start, MacLaren is frozen out of the biggest chunk. Which means he's really targeting the others.''

"And they are . . . ?''

"The next two largest holders are Harriet's stepchildren, David and Donna—Donna Palmer—who have about seventeen-plus percent each. David's president of the company, but that's pretty much a figurehead job. He has wanted more for years, but for my money, the guy's a loser. He's erratic, has a hot temper, plus a real fondness for the bottle. His wife, Carolyn, has far more brains and savvy than he does. Harriet would never let him run the company if she could prevent it.

"Donna, the stepdaughter, is pretty much out of the picture.'' Lon held the snifter to the light and squinted. "She's divorced, lives up in Boston, where she runs a public-relations firm. I don't think she's much interested in the paper, or in New York, for that matter."

"Is that all the family members who share in the ownership?"

"No, there's also Scott Haverhill, Harriet's nephew, with about ten precent. He's the general manager, and he wants the top spot about as badly as David does. He's an oily bastard, always trying to ingratiate himself with his aunt and maneuvering behind the scenes to weasel more power. She'd probably choose Scott over David to run the whole show, but only just barely. Lesser of two evils."

"You've accounted for about eighty percent of the ownership," Wolfe said, ringing for more beer. "The rest?"

"It's in smaller pieces," Lon said. "My boss, Carl Bishop, the publisher, has five percent, and he'd hold out against MacLaren till the finish. Elliot Dean, the family lawyer, who's been around for a hundred years, has about two or three percent, I think. He was a confidant of Wilkins Haverhill, and he's been Harriet's adviser since the old man died. A magazine publishing company, Arlen, has a piece, and so does a guy named Demarest, whose family sold the *Gazette* to Wilkins Haverhill."

Wolfe asked more questions about MacLaren, the *Gazette*, and the family, but you've already gotten the flavor. It was nearly eleven when Lon yawned, stretched, and lapped up the last of his fourth snifter of Remisier.

"I still don't know why you're so interested in that miserable Scotsman. But if anything I've said tonight gives you an innspiration about how to stop him, it will bring me more satisfaction that this meal has, which is saying a lot. Don't bother getting up, Archie, I'll see myself out."

I walked him to the front door anyway, partly because a guest in the brownstone is a jewel resting on a cushion of hospitality and partly because I feel better when I do the final bolting of the front door for the night myself. It's force of habit, spurred by the knowledge that there are at least ten people loose in Manhattan who would be more than happy to help arrange Nero Wolfe's funeral, not to mention a few who'd chip in to buy me a tombstone too.

When I walked back into the office, Wolfe was sitting upright, staring straight ahead, with his palms down on the desk.

"Archie, what does a full-page advertisement in the *Times* cost?"

"Beats me," I answered, raising one eyebrow and easing into my desk chair. "Well up in the thousands, I suppose. You planning a spectacular new way to solicit clients? A little showy, isn't it?"

He glared but said nothing, then closed his eyes. Because I have a thing about time. I checked my wrist and waited. After seven minutes, he woke up and blinked. "Instructions," he said.

"Yes, sir." I flipped open my notebook.

"Call the *Times* tomorrow morning and determine the cost of a full page. Let me know the price, although it will make little difference. Then go to their office and place the advertisement that—"

"What advertisement?"

"Don't interrupt! The advertisement that I'm about to give you. First, the headline, in forty-eight-point type . . ."

With that, he began dictating one of the most unusual messages a reader of the *Times* is ever likely to see. It took almost forty minutes, and he stopped occasionally to check a fact in his *World Almanac*. When he was done, I read my shorthand back to him, and he made a few minor changes.

"They won't print this," I ventured.

"I disagree. Through the years, the *Times* has run thousands of open letters and advocacy advertisements from individuals and organizations. It's part of their tradition. You like wagers, Archie; I'll be happy to give you odds they will accept it."

I grinned. "You're too confident; I pass."

"Make sure to keep a carbon when you type it," he said, getting up to go to bed. That was totally uncalled for. I always make carbons.

NERO WOLFE STEPS OUT

Every Wolfe Watcher knows that the world's largest detective wouldn't dream of leaving the brownstone on 35th street, with Fritz's three star meals, his beloved orchids and the only chair that actually suits him. But when an ultra-conservative college professor winds up dead and Archie winds up in jail, Wolfe is forced to brave the wilds of upstate New York to find a murderer.

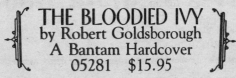

THE BLOODIED IVY
by Robert Goldsborough
A Bantam Hardcover
05281 $15.95

and don't miss these other Nero Wolfe mysteries by Robert Goldsborough:

☐ 27024 **DEATH ON DEADLINE** $3.95
            —FINALLY IN PAPERBACK!
☐ 26120 **MURDER IN E MINOR** $3.50

"A Smashing Success"—*Chicago Sun–Times*

And Bantam still offers you a whole series of Nero Wolfe mysteries by his creator, Rex Stout

☐ 24730 **DEATH OF A DUDE** $2.95
☐ 24918 **FER-DE-LANCE** $2.95
☐ 25172 **GAMBIT** $2.95
☐ 25425 **DEATH TIMES THREE** $2.95
☐ 25254 **FINAL DEDUCTION** $2.95

Look for them at your bookstore or use the coupon below:

Special Offer
Buy a Bantam Book
for only 50¢.

Now you can have Bantam's catalog filled with hundreds of titles plus take advantage of our unique and exciting bonus book offer. A special offer which gives you the opportunity to purchase a Bantam book for only 50¢. Here's how!

By ordering any five books at the regular price per order, you can also choose any other single book listed (up to a $5.95 value) for just 50¢. Some restrictions do apply, but for further details why not send for Bantam's catalog of titles today!

Just send us your name and address and we will send you a catalog!